Bolts From The Blue

By the same author

TO HEAVEN WITH SCRIBES AND PHARISEES
A BACKDOOR TO HEAVEN
A TASTE OF HEAVEN (with June Rose)
FORMS OF PRAYER (Two volumes:
    coeditor Rabbi Dr. J. Magonet)
BRIGHT BLUE
KITCHEN BLUES
SIMPLY DIVINE (with the Rev. John Eley)

Bolts From The Blue

Rabbi Lionel Blue

Hodder & Stoughton
LONDON SYDNEY AUCKLAND TORONTO

Illustrations by Albert Rusling

British Library Cataloguing in Publication Data

Blue, Lionel
  Bolts from the Blue.
  I. Title
  828'.91402   PR6052.L/

ISBN 0-340-37078-5

To Daphne Richardson, my friend

Contents

Introduction

People write to me, asking me to set down my theology and send it to them. And they mean business because they enclose a self-addressed envelope, stamped first class. I look at the envelope and feel confused because I don't have one special theology but several to suit my mood and this is the same as having none. This confusion does not keep me awake at night because my faith is not founded on any system about God, but some experiences of Him (or Her) and not very special ones at that.

They are the kind that happen to everybody. All of us at times are struck with awe, or horrified by evil, or melted by compassion, or invaded by love.

Many dismiss such experiences because they are fleeting, and because they have been brainwashed into believing that objects are real, and the spirit is insubstantial – it is not insubstantial, only invisible.

But religion, however solid and official, is based on such experiences. My own religion, with its committees, building funds and overdrafts, is founded on a dream of Jacob, Elijah's still small voice, and what Moses thought he saw in a burning bush. Such experiences are more substantial than they seem, for official religion has rested on them, securely enough, for four thousand years.

Cautiously, over the years, I have learned to trust them, and follow with hesitation where they lead. I trust my religion more readily because it surfaces in kitchens

9

and bus queues as well as in temples and on retreats. I prefer it when my common sense validates an uncommon one.

I have never exactly been 'converted' or 'born again' – I am not the type – but gradually my centre of gravity has shifted. Yes, I see the same world I saw before, but I see it in a different light. Some things which lay in shadow have begun to glow, and other things which seemed so important have become faded and dim. My values have started to turn inside out and now I locate my home in eternity as well as in a London suburb. It remains the same world but different.

Eventually serious people have to compose their own religious histories, the scriptures of their own lives – other scriptures about other people at other times, however grand, cannot replace them. These stories, incidents and conversations are the material for mine. Because they are 'mixed up' they are more credible, and their dotty inconsequential flavour has the hallmark of ordinary life – as she is lived by you and me. I hope they help you compose your own, for everyone has a scripture in them, whether published or not.

I don't set things down willingly, except under pressure, so I thank Robert Foxcroft, John Newbury, the *Today Programme*, *Manna* and other journals for getting me down to it and especial thanks to *The London Standard*, its editor, Mr Kirby, and their 'Bolts From The Blue'. Much of the material is the result of their stick and carrot and has appeared in those journals or been heard on the radio. I have therefore used a wide religious terminology as I have been talking to people of many faiths and of none.

My thanks to Tina and my mother, who prepared this manuscript, Janny and Eva who read it, and Jim and Guy who encouraged me to write it.

Teachers

At College I learned a lot about religion, but that wasn't enough. I needed to learn it, not just about it. You don't get this kind of learning from what your teachers say, but from what they are.

My real teachers, then, have been a motley crew. There were some rabbis among them certainly, but there were also beggars and businessmen, a bishop and bohemians, a tough Catholic 'Jewish' nun, and a dog.

Here are some notes on their teaching.

To have your bone and eat it

My dog Re'ach was a serious, contented animal who had a purpose in life. This purpose was centred on a lump of plastic, shaped and coloured to resemble a bloody beef chop, which squeaked when she bit it.

On summer mornings she waited impatiently until she could clock in at Kensington Gardens and get down to work. The gardens were thick with courting couples who lay prone, plastered together with dreamy desire. This my dog Re'ach was determined to destroy.

Bending over a girl who was sodden with sleep and love, she squeaked her chop. The girl, looking up, would see a black muzzle, a yard of wicked red tongue, and the bloody chop. Not unnaturally, she screamed. This aroused her swain from his deep dream of peace, and he would curse and Re'ach would squeak her chop defiantly until he rose up in wrath and Re'ach scampered away, well pleased with herself – another vigilante mission successfully accomplished, and not without danger.

This pastoral idyll could have gone on all summer, with the screams of girls and the squeak of chops, the oaths of swains and the woofs of dogs, as regular as the dawn chorus, a sort of pastoral silly symphony.

But in any Garden of Eden, a serpent lurks to rear its head. My American friend didn't look like a serpent. He was chubby and genial, and like many elderly

Americans, generous to a fault. Re'ach struck him as 'kinda cute', and as he was partial to chocolate chip ice cream and sweet Martini, which Re'ach kinda liked too, *'leur sublime s'amalgama'* – they shared the same ideal – as Saint-Simon so acutely observes of Archbishop Fénelon and Madame Guyon, his mystic guide.

To increase her contentment, though contentment is content with itself and needs no increase, as my American friend should have known, he presented pooch with a plastic squealing bone to complement her squeaking chop. Re'ach gazed at the bone besotted, and when she bit it and found out it squealed, she ran around the garden again and again, intoxicated by the quantity and the quality of her possessions.

She squeaked her chop but then had to let it go to pick up her bone. She then squealed her bone and let it go to pick up her chop. Neither action felt right for she wanted both, and she made a frantic attempt to hold both her chop and her bone at the same time but her jaws, alas, could not cope.

Her contentment had gone. When she held one, the memory of the other would surface in the murk of her mind, and her grief over what she did not have spoilt the pleasure of what she did. It was an existential problem as Sartre could have told her and Simone de Beauvoir too. But Re'ach was not a philosophical dog, so she sat back on her haunches and howled at the tragedy of life. It was too much.

I thought of her as I sat in the synagogue. The rabbi was chanting the scriptures from the scroll and the words were uncompromising: 'See I have set before you this day life and good, and death and evil . . . Choose life . . .' (Deut. 30:15,19).

Now Re'ach would not have liked that. She wanted to have her bone and eat it. And sometimes when I think of all that has to be given up for the sake of eternal life, I

don't like it either. And I too, would like to sit back on my
haunches and howl.

Colin

She was old and derelict, her shoes squelched water and
she had wrapped some newspapers under her blouse for
warmth. She clung to my jacket and tried to bully me into
buying a dud bracelet. It was New Year's Eve and I was
in a pub celebrating. I fished out eighty pence from my
pocket and put the coins on the table next to her.

Why? Well, if you're religious, you have to live with an
itchy conscience. Also she reminded me of my grandma.
Also I thought I might end up like that, and the money
was a kind of insurance. Also I wanted to buy her off as I
am fastidious.

Having done my duty, I moved away sharply with my
glass to the other end of the bar where I could relax.
While I sipped away, I suddenly thought of Colin whom
I hadn't thought about for years. You may have heard of
him too, because before his death he became Bishop of
Damaraland-in-exile, who celebrated communion in
Trafalgar Square with hot gospel choirs.

When I got to know him at Oxford, the future bishop
was flogging undies and cut-price nylons and what have
you in the market during the vacation with my other
mates, for all of us were up at Oxford on austerity grants.

Though I was revolutionary and Colin was religious,
we decided to hitch-hike to Israel together, for ladies'
lingerie was a link between us. Colin wanted to inspect
relics and I wanted to witness revolutions, not the kind
that was cooked up and then fizzled out in Oxford Junior
Common Rooms.

We lurched across Europe, squeezed on to trucks, and got scarred for life on the top of gravel lorries. It was a relief when a hearse unexpectedly stopped for us in Burgundy. As the stately hearse seemed to be just right for religion, with my consent Colin had a go at converting me from Trotsky to the Church of England, but it was too big a jump and he hadn't yet had enough missionary practice. He lectured me on the apostolic succession. It seemed to be a chancy thing like all life's goodies.

Some people had it, and some had just missed the boat. Colin was sure the Church of England had it, and he thought the Church of Sweden might have it too, transmitted by a Swedish Bishop of the Reformation who Colin freely admitted, was bonkers.

I put up with it because I had a Talmudic mind. But if Colin didn't teach me doctrine, he taught me some real religion. I was always losing things. Now, a lot of ethical people will lend you their toothpaste, but Colin lent me his toothbrush as well, and his least dirty socks and his sleeping-bag. I don't suppose all Anglican bishops are like that, which is understandable but a pity.

We finally went steerage on an old crock of a boat to the Holy Land. The Officers told us to get off by the first class gangway and being prudent, that is what I did, but

16

Colin refused. So a nice lassie welcomed me to the Holy Land with a cup of iced malted milk. Sipping it, I watched Colin come down with the ragtag and bobtail. He waved to me snootily and then disappeared like Moses in a cloud because someone stuck a nozzle down his shirt and deloused him. He looked a bit crestfallen, but I didn't say 'I told you so' because I realised then that he had a religious quality I lacked. I disliked poverty, but I didn't like poor people. Colin not only liked them, he tried to love their poverty as well.

Looking across the bar I saw the old lady move somebody's abandoned glass in front of her, so that she could pretend to be a bona fide drinker and enjoy the smoky warmth till closing time. Thinking of Colin I ordered two pints of bitter and took them over to her table. 'We'll drink to old friends', I said and she blearily assented. It was better than a memorial prayer, and it seemed a sacramental way to start the New Year.

Louis and Lottie

I first met her about twenty years ago. She was clothed in a black bombazine pup tent and on her head she wore a stiff starched white creation, like the frills on lamb chops, though she was not lamb but tough mutton.

With a slight guttural accent, she informed me her name was Sister Louis Gabriel, which seemed improbable as she remained a German-Jewish refugee to the end of her days.

She also didn't look at me directly but averted her eyes, which made her appear shifty. Perhaps she was overcome, I thought, at meeting a real rabbi and felt guilty about her conversion to Christianity.

I underestimated her completely. She had seen her synagogue set on fire in Berlin. She had married unsuccessfully, and fallen in love successfully. She had also fallen into the arms of the Church, and since she did nothing by halves, became a Catholic nun in Jewish Jerusalem teaching Arab children. She had been rescued by an Italian princess who had shipped her to Palestine, and there she had worked for British Intelligence. Having faced Nazis, Fascists, and clerical disapproval, one immature rabbi was nothing to her. Being shifty wasn't in her nature; she was just being thorough and old time and keeping custody of her eyes.

She told me she disapproved of converts. People should stay in the religion where God had put them.

I swallowed hard, and said gravely, 'Except you of course.'

'Of course,' she answered without batting an eyelid.

I saw Sister Louis Gabriel some years later after she came back from America. 'I am no longer called Louis,' she announced, 'but Lottie, my birth name.'

Sister Lottie was into liberation theology from Central America and wore long pants which she had battled for at a Harrods sale.

She was as thoroughly modern as Sister Louis had been old time. She puffed at a cigarette in a long holder while she sipped a weak whisky 'on the rocks'.

'Lionel, why don't you have a highball?' she said.

'Louis,' I said, 'no, Lottie, what on earth happened to your habit?'

'Hm . . . Let them use it for demonstrations,' she said. She also gave me a book she had written about anti-Jewish prejudice in the Church. It didn't surprise me that she wasn't the establishment's favourite nun. It was a courageous book which said things that needed saying and only Louis/Lottie could have said them. Being a German-Jewish refugee was tough. Being a German-

18

Jewish refugee who became a Catholic nun was even tougher.

She taught me that religion was not about security or popularity, it was about courage, and witnessing to the truth as you knew it, not as someone else had told you you ought to know it. She was the only person I've ever met who could interrupt a sermon and say, 'Father, this is not so!' – something I've always wanted to do but never dared.

I used to collect refugee jokes for Charlotte and saved this one for her, a version of which I had heard from her friend Rabbi Gryn.

Two Jewish refugees in Milwaukee debated as to how you pronounced it. Was it Milwaukee or Milvaukee? In the synagogue they asked a warden which of them was right.

'Oh, it's Milvaukee,' he said.

'Thank you,' they replied.

'You're velcome.'

Before I could tell it to her she died. Jesuits and Dominicans said a requiem Mass for her. Rabbis said Kaddish for her, and Sisters and unbelievers, addicts and the alcoholics she had helped, mourned for her.

The Sister had guts!

Anneliese's guru hunt

My friend Anneliese, who had built a religious conference centre and retreat house in Germany, was looking for someone to do a repair job on her own faith, which had started to come apart during the war.

Though middle-aged when I met her, she still had the eager innocence of a child, and I agreed to join her in a guru hunt, as I also liked salvation in different flavours.

One of the gurus said that God was dead but most agreed He was alive and lived in them exclusively. Some of them said they lived in Him. Perhaps this was the same thing, and perhaps it wasn't. Anneliese and I couldn't figure it out. One lady told us she was God and asked for a double portion of Anneliese's chocolate pudding. Anneliese was a bit shirty about this, but after all rank has its privileges.

Anneliese told me she had read about a guru who knew God's telephone number, though when you rang it there was never any reply. The guru said, 'What else

do you expect?' Anneliese and I considered this remark over a bottle of Moselle and decided it wasn't unreasonable and might be quite profound.

Anneliese eventually found a super spiritual teacher who didn't fancy himself as God, though he was, thank

God, a gentleman. He wasn't only holy, he was polite. Well, she confiscated him immediately and lured by her goodness and the prospect of endless meditation in comfy surroundings with good food and central heating he drove us back to her retreat house. He was as eager as a puppy to bust into the beyond. So eager that as he speeded along the Autobahn he started to meditate on the names of God before we got there. There were, I think, about ninety-nine, but I didn't count, as he half-closed his eyes while reciting them and lifted his hands from the steering wheel in supplication. Anneliese had a direct religious experience and I had never felt closer to eternity.

I agreed with Anneliese her centre could do with more spiritual tone and suggested a live-in hermit. I had forgotten how literal Anneliese could be in the German manner. When I came again I found she had filched a real hermit from a real monastery. She had constructed for him a purpose-built cell on a neighbouring alp and had also thoughtfully provided a large alsatian. The hermit could love the dog and the faithful dog would protect him. Both seemed to me rather lonely on their eyrie and I suspect had had enough of each other. The dog had no vocation for a solitary life and the nice plucky hermit, for all his spiritual horsepower, could have done, I thought, with a pint in a pub.

Eventually Anneliese settled back in the bosom of her own church, which I agreed was the best thing. Why did she ever go on a guru hunt, for she was such a competent, practical woman, such a brilliant fund raiser? 'Because I feel guilty,' she said. 'I should have ended up in a concentration camp and I didn't.' Still, she had built a refuge for women in distress, and a house for refugees. She aided the German refugees fleeing from their land in the East which had been occupied. She also sent food parcels to the Poles who were occupying it. She made a home for apprehensive Jews, starving students, and forlorn Turkish guest workers. She had been grilled by the Gestapo and had adopted thirteen children without any money. She made Germany pure for me – she was my own Deutsche Yiddisher mamma, my buxom blessed Brunhilde, my loving Lorelei.

She died about the same time as Sister Louis, whom she liked and respected. I hope she now realises what I always knew and tried to tell her: that all the faith she sought on earth was already quite safe inside her.

'1,000 she-asses'

I have always been partial to happy endings – really happy endings when the boy and girl get each other and a lot of money as well, and it all happens by moonlight in Monte Carlo. I don't like clever endings when the couple do come together but only in death. It's not easy to find my type of ending in any respectable cinema or theatre nowadays and as well as the gloom-and-doom brigade, intellectuals look down on it also.

This used to worry me and I wondered if I was immature. So, many years ago, on the continent, along with other priests and pastors who also wanted to grow up, I went to all sorts of seminars and lectures on relationships. They did help a lot but my escapism was immediately visible. Did we lock our bathroom door against our own children? we were asked searchingly! Well, I didn't have any, but my bathroom was, and is, closed to all comers. Black mark, Blue!

At another place we were asked to locate our inner aggression. Though I normally have lots of the stuff, I couldn't find it when I wanted it, only sweet and sticky love. My colleagues, though, were getting full marks for locating all sorts of nastiness inside themselves.

Finally we were given a treat and allowed to cut our teeth on case histories – hypothetical ones of course, as we were not strong enough for the real thing. They were very sad and went rather like this:

> Miss X is on the bottle – but not like the one her mother gave her as a baby, more like the ones her father stashes away. He is grouchy because Master X, Miss X's brother, sports a diamond in his left ear and Miss X's fiancé is on the needle not the bottle. Overcome by all this, Miss X's mother is shopping around for cut-price glue in the High Street. Was it any wonder that Miss X weeps into her bridal chest as she plans her trousseau and has another snort.

What was our advice? We recommended therapy of every sort – Freudian, Jungian, Kleinian and National Health in all its continental complexity. We finally suggested prayer and got a sniff. Someone suggested a primal scream and got beamed at. Another suggested aversion therapy and got slapped down.

Finally an old and silent minister was asked to comment, for the old must be encouraged, you know.

'I would ring Mr Y,' he said, after much thought.

'Oh, Mr Y is a social worker?' asked our leader.

'No,' he said. 'Old Y knows nothing from nothing – except panties, of course. He manufactures them,' he added helpfully. 'But he's generous with his panty profits and I'd ask him for some to send this poor young lady to a good hotel at the seaside. Some smoked salmon inside her would buck her up and who knows,' and his eyes gleamed, 'she might meet a nice young accountant or dentist, and this dreadful story would have a happy ending.'

I looked at him with admiration. Happy endings aren't easy to come by, but that doesn't mean we should give up too easily. You may think you want a vocation, when all you need is a vacation.

Take up your Bible. After his argument with God Job didn't end up very poor. 'The Lord blessed Job,' it says, with '14,000 sheep, 6,000 camels and 1,000 she-asses' – and that's a lot of sheep and she-asses.

And the gospels end surprisingly and delightfully with a fried-fish barbecue at the seaside. Look it up for yourself in the last chapter of St John.

Family Faith

Some parts of my life seem barren as I look back on them and others call me back again and again, yielding new treasure every time I consider those years. My perception of the worlds – this one and the next – was formed at a very early age. For a while I thought I had lost this perception and it took me a long time to recover it, but the inheritance of my grandparents and parents was always there, awaiting rediscovery. It determined long ago my attitude to poverty and purpose, beggars and holiness, food and faith – which is a lot.

There is an old Jewish fable which says that before you are born an angel tells you what your life will be about. Then he strikes you with a little hammer (this accounts for the crease between your eyes above your nose) and you forget it. But throughout life, when you encounter something significant it always seems as if you just remembered it, not learned it.

That is the way it feels with my family inheritance.

My inheritance

A lot of my attitudes come from my granny and grandpa. They came to this country as children from Russia. My granny's parents had died in a pogrom and the people in her village put a paper round her neck with her name and clubbed together to buy her steerage ticket to London. There, it was said, she had an uncle who wore a gold watch and chain and ate chicken twice a week. My grandfather was a young lad fleeing from conscription to Siberia and hopefully trying to get to America. In fact, when he landed here, he thought it was America and only discovered the truth some years afterwards, but by that time it was too late. He had married Granny (as they never knew their age, I wonder what birth dates they gave to the marriage registrar) and had set up as a cobbler near the docks in London. I don't think Granny ever worked out where she was.

I learned to swear in Polish, Russian and Yiddish from Grandpa. I have not the slightest idea still what the words mean, but I once tried them out, experimentally, at an international conference. You read about someone's jaw dropping, but have you ever seen it? Well, I have.

I also learned from him how to make a good breakfast. He wasn't into cereals and fruit juice, but black bread, raw onions, pickled herring and Russian tea laced with lemon and rum.

They left me a strange inheritance. It didn't consist of goods, because they hardly had any, and the little they had was blown up in the Blitz. It consisted of a bundle of attitudes I have never been able to change.

Granny, like many Eastern people, thought beggars were holy, and I was always instructed to give a small coin to every one I met because they were the closest we ever got to meeting God. This still makes a walk down Oxford Street torture. I have to provide myself with a bag

of change, and the policemen get suspicious because I am constantly crossing to the other side of the street. Not being as generous as Granny, I try to walk down Wigmore Street instead. My fellow pedestrians there might feel down and low (all those psychiatrists lurking around Harley Street) but they are certainly not down and out, so I can still afford a cup of coffee by the time I get to Marble Arch.

I used to know an old beggar woman over thirty years ago when I studied at the Seminary in Upper Berkeley Street. She completed my religious education by telling me sharp truths my professors didn't know or didn't care to communicate. She once confessed her sins publicly in a local church and it brought the house down. She was ejected because they sounded far too lush.

I never got too near her, because she scratched a lot, but when I proffered a coin with an outstretched arm she burst into fits of laughter at my timidity.

'Don't worry, dearie,' she cackled. 'I'll open a bank account, and that will let you off the hook nicely.'

Thank God Granny wasn't there for she would have spotted the calculation in my charity and my coldness of heart. I could not have stood it.

According to Granny's lights

A friend of mine told me she was going to a high-class cookery school in London, and I brooded over it. The students would be called Samantha or Jeremy. They would be clean within and without. They would wrap this and that up in juicy spinach leaves and stew them in kiwi juice. This and that would be presented, not served, on dear and austere white bone china, with a discreet gold rim to hint that a heart of gold is just not enough.

I say all this out of envy, because I, too, would like to cook in ramekins and have thoughts as pure as my china. But, alas, I learned cookery in a different school. Grandma's kitchen did not have a food processor, and there was not even a bath for our bodies, let alone a bain marie for crème caramel. (Like the rest of the genteel upper-crust of Stepney we queued at the public baths, once a week before Sabbath.)

She had instead a cauldron, an axe, a block and a barrel. There were clean rags to staunch the blood if you were absent-minded and split your artery. She couldn't sift or blanch, but she had a way with bones and those parts of an animal other gourmets never reach and which belong more to the study of anatomy than cookery.

Many years later, when I read history at Balliol, I tried to imagine medieval battlefields and they came alive as I remembered Grandma's kitchen with the wallop of the axe and the splintering of her bones.

Her weekend triumph was to stuff a lung and roast it. It was certainly cheap and looked like grey polystyrene. Only after the depression years ended did I learn, to my surprise, that Sunday roasts need not have holes like meaty honeycomb.

She also knew how to keen over her cauldron, and this is a lost art. It is fashionable now in Hampstead and Highgate to urge on flowers with pretty chat or co-counsel with your herbs. This I can accept quite easily because Grandma at heart was more animist than Jewish. Like a Viking, she denounced her axe in ringing tones when it did not dismember as it should, and if the lung was too dry, and came out more like breeze block than delicate polystyrene, she wept over it, like Jeremiah amid the ruins of Jerusalem.

In her school, I was not a complete success. I never learned to cut spaghetti safely with an axe, and I would as soon roast a pillow as a lung, though they have the same shape and size. But I absorbed a mine of misinformation or unproved information – that fish would give me brains, and carrots would help me see in the dark, and garlic would take away the evil eye. I once gave a sermon against superstition when I was a theological student. The congregation was edified and I was mortified when I instinctively walked round a ladder, not underneath it, after the service. That was Granny!

But never mind, she taught me generosity, because she would get up at night, and taking me with her, waddle round the block in her great black shawl. She put little parcels of food in the doorways of the unemployed, the needy, or the refugees. She did it at night because she was a lady and instinctively knew that giver and receiver should never meet.

The spirit was alive and well in her valley of dead bones.

Say it with whelks

A lot of people feel guilty about having a temper. You can't always sublimate it or suppress it. Sometimes you just have to express it and get it out of your system.

Take the case of my mother. In her youth she worked as a pianist for the silent films. She sat on a bench underneath the screen and, craning her neck, tried to match the characters with musical composition. It was not a classy cinema, only a flea-pit, and my mother's repertoire was limited.

When she saw the heroine she played 'Hearts and Flowers'. She knew three other tunes, one each for the hero and the villain, and she banged out the overture to *Zampa* for the Keystone Cops and any other rough-house on the screen. The hours were long, the times were hard, and the pay was poor. When my mother fell asleep, or, bemused by the flickering lights, played the wrong tune, the audience pelted her with peanuts – if she were lucky – and whelks if she weren't.

They, too, had their grievances for they were packed

on to benches without dividers. As more were crammed in at one end, more fell off at the other, and sometimes one end rose in the air and a rough-house took place off the screen as well as on it.

My mother, who was nicely brought up and only rouged her knees like any decent girl when her mother, my grandmother, wasn't around, endured it as long as she could, coming home every day in tears.

My grandma could not abide this droopiness. My mother's sniffing spoilt her tea. My father, too, who had been eyeing her for some time, secretly wondered if she were too damp for him. Grandpa tried to shame her into dryness and told her to go back to Russia, where she would have something to cry about. To strengthen her, Grandma made her a bowl of strong chicken soup – the classic Jewish standby. But my mother wept into it, reducing its strength.

My uncle, who was built like a six-foot gorilla, and a fighter, finally took a hand. He filled a bag with chicken bones and stale strudel and taught my mother how to

play *Zampa* with one hand and throw the contents with the other. He went with her to the cinema to urge her on.

Under his instruction, my mother never looked back. The first whelk hit her while the heroine was renouncing true love. My mother, nervous but excited, replied with a chicken bone and a squelchy tomato. What followed was the roughest house the flea-pit had ever known. Once Ma had discarded her maidenly inhibitions everything went with it, including the piano stool, which caused havoc among the peanut fanciers.

She returned home battered but triumphant, and talk had replaced tears. The rest of the family just couldn't shut her up as she analysed the missiles and the strategies she had used. She glowed with clean emotion, and my father impulsively asked her out on a date (with a chaperone, of course). As she no longer sniffed he proposed to her and I was the result.

Now religious people have a lot of trouble with temper. They bottle it up and make themselves unreal. Or, they turn it inwards and give themselves migraines. Or, they disguise it with concern and it comes out as righteous indignation. I do not know how this disowning of temper came into religion. It is certainly not there in the Bible. God and His people are constantly having a go at each other. The exchanges get quite nasty. But the nice thing is that they are able to make it up, and, apart from occasional recriminations, enjoy each other again. This is what it means to be long-suffering – having a temper, yes, but letting it poison you, no. And this isn't just Old Testament stuff, it's in the New as well. After all, look up St Matthew's Gospel and read what Jesus said to the fig tree!

Making up rows

A newspaper rang me up and asked me to recall my childhood memories of the religious festivals we celebrated at home. 'Yes,' I replied, 'I have some very strong memories. I remember especially the rows we used to have.' 'Oh,' said the voice at the other end, 'what were they about?'

Well, our rows weren't about Jewish law or tradition or something dignified like that. A lot of them were about my alleged debauchery, which was pretty thick as I was only five at the time.

I'd better explain.

My mother and my aunts wanted us to behave like a model Jewish family, the kind you see in the teaching manuals. They wanted us to look holy and wholesome like the contented families on the backs of cereal packets who grinned over their grapefruit. But my grandparents were not into cornflakes and grapefruit. They had stronger tastes. What they liked was raw onions, rows and rumpus.

'Hetty,' my grandfather would say to my mother, leaning over the festival table, fed up with playing happy families. 'You are debauching that child with alcohol.'

'But Daddy,' shrieked my mother, rising to the bait, 'I was only giving him a spoonful of festival wine.'

Granny, scenting delight and danger, started keening away at her end of the table. 'He,' she said, pointing at Grandpa with a spoon, 'is cruel like a Cossack.' She groaned and peered upwards as if locating the Almighty near the flypaper. 'An oppressor of his own flesh and blood.'

She and Grandpa smiled contentedly and let battle commence.

My mother, who had caught on by now, decided her strong suit was pathos. 'The babe,' she whispered, 'the poor ignorant babe.'

This I bitterly resented.

'What will his inheritance be from such grandparents as these?' My grandmother nodded approvingly and munched a pickled cucumber.

There was a walk-out, blessings mixed with blistering home truths, a come-back and more wine, given to me this time, debauched as I was, by Grandpa himself, and really a lovely celebration was had by all.

We were purged by catharsis, as Aristotle would have put it, though none of us knew this at the time because we didn't know any Greeks.

All this was followed by another row about my alleged debauchery.

Grandpa took me to see the *Merchant of Venice* in Yiddish. The theatre was in uproar over the love scene between Lorenzo and Jessica. The Yiddish audience did not see it as a comedy. Here was the daughter of a pious Jew disgracing herself shamelessly on a public stage with a self-confessed Gentile. My grandfather this time was upbraided for debauching me and there was an awful row. His defence, that it was art and educational, was scornfully pushed aside.

But everyone made it up and agreed that it was an interesting evening, even though *Abbie's Irish Rose*, which had a similar theme, was more genteel and artistic.

Such rows never could debauch me for I learned early on that where there are two Jews there are three opinions. And the scriptures bear this out, for they tell the story of the rumpus between the prophets, the Almighty and the Children of Israel which has never stopped.

My grandparents were unsophisticated folk, but they knew that in most rows you are arguing with part of your own self. It is your own doubts you are suppressing. Unless you make up, you may hurt others but you will certainly maim yourself as well. They never left me any goods to inherit because they didn't have many, but they tried to show me by example in early childhood how to have a holy row, and make it up, and how to resolve a religious conflict with decency.

Grandma's voice

Many people's religion is not centred on a book or a theology, nor on an organisation or a tradition. For Granny and myself such things came later, for though wonderful, they are also hand-me-downs from other people at other times. The centre of our religion is a conversation with a voice. My Granny thought her voice was outside her, and I imagine my voice inside me. But the difference is only fashion. Of course being educated, unlike her, I've wondered if the voice were just my own reflection, but after a long analysis I can assure you it isn't. Also, the voice itself over the years does not deny my common sense, it just completes it, that's all, with an uncommon one.

I pieced together Granny's personal religion from odd bits of family history. My father was the eldest of her children – there were about fourteen and she couldn't bear to be separated from any of them. So when my father was called up in the First World War his mother came too. He was sent from barracks to barracks and Grandma followed him with all her other children, and a complete kitchen with one set of pots and pans for milk and another for meat. She was frightened my father might breakfast off eggs and rashers of damnation if she weren't around, and she certainly had a point. These pious campfollowers caused great hilarity on barrack squares all over the country and my father nearly died of shame.

Anyway, that is how the family happened to arrive in Ireland just in time for the revolution. I'm rather hazy as to what took place there, because neither my father nor Granny could speak of it calmly. He was ardent for King and country, because he had once taken a day trip to Ostend and personally felt for gallant little Belgium.

Grandma's opinions were on the other side, though my father said she wasn't entitled to an opinion, only a prejudice, for she couldn't understand a word of Irish, or English for that matter, only White Russian and Yiddish, and she had never been enlightened by a day trip to Ostend. Gran had come from *Fiddler-on-the-Roof* country, and in Ireland the same sort of piety prevailed, outweighing the prevalence of pigs, of which she thought there were far too many.

Everybody over there was chatting up God. The Protestants sang psalms to Him ceaselessly and the Catholics shmoozed Him up at their shrines. Now that was real religion, and Granny approved.

And so do I, because I converse with God, though I give one warning to all who like to chat with the cosmos. You can talk so much that God can't get a word in edgeways, and so your piety won't improve you or revive you. That's the trouble with a lot of religion, whether it's English, Jewish, Irish or whatever. But if you've chatted with God all your life, you do get to know him as you know a friend or a father. So like Granny I'm not afraid of death, though I don't like pain, because I'm curious to meet at last the Being whose voice I've conversed with for nearly forty years.

When I was in Ireland, a priest told me this story which would have suited Granny fine, if he could have told it in White Russian. Two workers were repairing a church roof. Looking down, one of them saw below an old lady. Winking to his mate, his voice boomed down, 'Bridy Murphy.' The old lady never looked up, so his friend joined in: 'Bridy Murphy,' he intoned. Again the old lady below didn't seem to hear. Exasperated, they both boomed down: 'Bridy Murphy.'

The old lady looked up with a sigh. 'Can't you please keep quiet for a few minutes now, while I'm having a chat with your mother!'

I was once asked, 'What God do I really worship?' And I answered, 'The God of my fathers, of course.'

Well, for accuracy I'd better amend that statement and say, 'I worship the God of my paternal grandmother, and for the same reason she did.'

'A smoothy'

One of the professional hazards of religion is becoming a 'smoothy'. If you don't say the right banalities you don't get invited to the right banquets. My gown, which is like a black bombazine tent, hides my bulge, my sex and my humanity. If I speak from a pulpit, no one contradicts me, even when I'm wrong, and neither of these conditions makes for honesty. Although religion is good at truth it isn't that good at honesty. It has some wonderful things to say about love, for example, and some quite silly things to say about sex.

Fortunately for my spiritual health I come from an outspoken family who never hesitated to say exactly what they thought. My grandfather just said out loud

38

whatever popped into his mind. I remember going along with him once to offer condolences to our relations – an elderly aunt of his had died. Grandpa said soothingly to the startled mourners, 'I know just how you feel, I hate losing things.' I remember as I left with him the glazed look in their eyes as they watched us go. On the way home Grandpa gave me a homily on tact and the comforting of the bereaved.

He didn't make this remark out of spite, because he was a loving man, even if he had endured a lot from the aunt in question. She was a formidable old lady who wrote out all her bills in Yiddish poetry and was determined to save Grandpa's soul at whatever inconvenience to her and especially to him.

We used to go and visit her on the Sabbath. Before Grandpa could enter the door she insisted he open his mouth while she smelt his breath. While the neighbours peeked out of the windows she examined his teeth (rather like examining a horse) for telltale strands of tobacco. She was a traditionalist so smoking was out on the Sabbath as was money, travelling, working and cooking. But Sabbath was not a grim day. There was a samovar going, which gave out a constant stream of hot tea, and sex was definitely in.

Jewish married couples were supposed to 'be fruitful and multiply' on Friday night if the purity laws permitted. My grandparents had an enormous brass bedstead, the like of which I have only seen since in Italy. Above it was their marriage contract, signed and framed, as evidence of their respectability and permission from on High to do whatever they did in the eyes of God and man. There was also a brown mezzotint of the Infant Samuel, a highly coloured and unsettling picture of Moses, with the incidents from his life depicted carefully in the background. I personally would not care to make love under the ten plagues, but what is pious to one generation is kinky to the next.

On the way home from the wake, Grandpa used to regale me with such stories as he considered suitable for my age and condition. Quite often I never got the point, but this one I always remembered.

A woman's husband died, and the undertakers carried the coffin carefully down the stairs. As they got to an awkward bend, the coffin slipped and crashed against the wall. As the bearers rushed to pick it up, they heard a faint cry within. Quickly they broke open the lid and revived the poor man. They carried him upstairs to his flat, and gave him a spoonful of brandy. Well, he recovered and lived contentedly for another year, when he died again.

As the coffin was taken once more down the stairs and got to the bend, his wife piped up in a tremulous tone, 'Be very, very careful! At this very spot, a terrible accident took place only a year ago.'

I remembered it because what amazed me at the time was why Grandpa hadn't told it to the mourners – just to cheer them up and comfort them.

As I have about the same amount of tact as Grandpa, life hasn't been that smooth, but at least when I pray I don't just butter up the Almighty, I occasionally tell Him what I really think.

'And his mother came too!'

My mother is a genial character who takes a high view of God and a low one of her fellow worshippers. Religion with a small 'r' she likes; religion with a capital 'R' is, she thinks, for the leisured classes, who play bridge and golf and still have time left over. It wasn't intended for working women like her. After all, when did she ever have time to make and donate little pots of chutney, and fairy biscuits?

I can vouch for that. As a child I remember her galloping home from work (she was a secretary) and never having time to change, so there she would stand in a swagger overcoat, with an evil little fox draped round her neck, biting its own tail. It had nasty eyes, and I was frightened of it. Occasionally a paw or tail dropped into the soup pot and had to be squeezed out.

In her hand she waved a long cigarette holder, which was a relic of her flapper days when she was a Stepney Charleston Queen and rouged her knees. She only pretended to smoke, in short little puffs, because she never knew how to handle the smoke, which made her choke.

She has always been an intrepid woman, who would try her hand at anything, and indeed lend her hand to anything or anybody. For example, her boss gave her a machine for making juices, for he was fastidious and vegetarian. Ma thought the carrots weren't going round fast enough in the machine, so to help them on she stuck her finger in, the top of which got juiced with the carrots. Covering the mutilated member with a napkin, she managed to serve the juice and make it back to the office kitchen before she fainted. In hospital she came to for a few minutes. 'Thank God,' she muttered, 'it was carrots not spinach, the colour . . . so lucky . . .' She then passed out again. All this happened in the thirties when jobs were hard to find. I don't think her boss ever knew what a potent brew he drank.

The only time we took against each other was when I was up at Oxford. My mother had come to visit me unexpectedly. I told her indulgently that I was now at the centre of a social whirl and could not spare the time to look after her. 'Have a cup of cocoa at the tearooms,' I said kindly, 'and take a book to bed.' She assured me she would be no trouble.

When I got to the party an excited student rushed out to welcome me. 'Lionel', he said, 'come and meet an extraordinary woman Jeremy picked up at the Randolph bar.' Well, I was introduced to my own mother, and, moodily, I left, since possession is nine points of the law.

Though she still doesn't go for formal religion, she taught me a lot which helped me professionally. Some of it was practical. Whenever I wore my robes I used to trip up, and this shattered the pious atmosphere of the services I was conducting. Ma showed me how she glided upstairs in an evening dress, and I have never since fallen flat while praying. But she also taught me not to whine in prayers. You didn't beg heaven for happiness, you just asked for a little help to make your own. After all, life isn't that bad! As she pointed out, look how lucky she was because it was carrots not spinach, and she kept her job! After all, jobs didn't grow on trees, but fingers grew again. How very lucky!

Prayer

I never started to pray because I was told to, and never continued to pray because I ought to. I pray out of enjoyment and need. Enjoyment, because it gives my life the only grandeur it possesses. Need because after I have let my own neurotic fluff settle down, I begin to see the next step ahead, not the step after the next – I must emphasise this – only the next.

Over the years, through prayer, I have become friendly with God. You only get to friendship with any being, animal, human or divine, by talking to them, and sitting with them in silence.

It has taken me a lifetime to trust in these meetings – it didn't come easily.

Is prayer like a cigarette?

Some disasters you can't do much about. If you've put cayenne pepper instead of paprika in the goulash, soap powder instead of soup powder in the stew, there's no point in covering it with garlic or vanilla. Chuck it, and get out your tin opener. If you bury the cans in the compost heap, and their contents under enough parsley, who's going to know? Though they'll suspect.

But you don't often use soap powder instead of soup powder – at least not more than once or twice a year – and the usual kitchen disasters are more borderline. What

'Anyone for Lincolnshire fen?'

happens with them depends on your conviction, not your cooking. A fallen soufflé is just a risen omelette. It depends on how you look at it, that's all – from above or below. And if the Yorkshire pudding's gone cold, slice it and butter it, and if you haven't got the nerve to call it Scotch pancakes, well then, call the slices by a different county in the same vicinity – Cumberland cuts, for example, or Northumberland nightmares.

Provided you say firmly enough, 'Have a nice Northumberland nightmare', your guests will only say how much nicer it is than that silly old Yorkshire pudding you meet simply everywhere.

My dog Re'ach was impressionable like that. The taste was all in her mind, which she didn't have much of. She used to stand by her dog bowl at mealtimes and watch me narrowly for my reaction. If I didn't show any interest in its contents, it was dust and ashes to her. If I made a move to snatch it, then the same dust was fit for a dog's dinner, and she woofed it before I could get near it. Once she didn't get there fast enough and I stuck my face in a bowl of soya, flavoured with artificial rabbit.

But you are doubtless thinking 'We want rabbi not rabbit, mate! Give us your message and get on with it!'

Well, there are disasters in life like cayenne or soap powder, and it's no use pretending they are anything else. When you lose a loved one, for example, there's no silver lining to cover the grief.

But most situations in life are not like that. They are more like the soufflé or the Yorkshire pud. It depends on how you take them whether they become delights or disasters, jokes or tragedies. That's why, when they happen, praying is so important.

Practically speaking, prayer helps you like a cigarette – but without the nasty side effects – because it allows you to pause. And in that pause is protection, because you have time to ask yourself what your problem is trying to tell you, what God is saying to you in it. Perhaps there is a blessing wrapped up in there, if you stop panicking.

The world God created has strange properties. It acts like a mirror, reflecting your feelings back to you. If you gaze into the world with trust, then life justifies that trust. If you look into it with hate, then it is indeed hateful, for your problems are not only in the world but also in you. And though God will not change the world for you, He has given you the tools to change yourself, and you are part of the world.

But I'm not going to labour the point. Here's a little Jewish story to relax with, after all this metaphysic. Don't take it too heavy, dearie, or pull it apart to get the message, because it hasn't got one.

As Mrs Levy was buying food in the market for the Bank Holiday, she shouted to Mrs Cohen, 'Oy, oy, Mrs Cohen, vot a big haddock I've got.' And Mrs Cohen replied, 'Hev a hesprin, Mrs Levy, here's a hesprin. Hits a hentidote!'

'Not tonight I've got a headache'

Now, as I've said before, you can either grin or groan. Down on your knees and meditate on it. It's over to you.

Substitute for love

A lady wrote to me, asking if I could help her because her great love was ending. It was horrible, she said, like watching television and seeing all the colour drain out of it. Could religion help her?

Well, I'll try not to cheat and I'll be both religious and realistic, for though it's not easy to keep them together, it's a cop-out if you don't try. Yes, my dear, unless somebody else happens with indecent haste, the sadness is going to stay around for quite a while, and religion won't solve your loss, only help you to live with it.

But it's not fatal. People die of famine, not love – at least, in all my years as a minister, I've only seen it happen to a dog, not a human being.

It's going to be tough living on your own. The same plates you didn't wash up in the morning will stare at you when you come back, and cooking for one isn't easy and at first you might burst into tears over your chop.

But there's still no need to take it that heavy, dear. A love affair isn't the purpose of your life on earth, and sex isn't all that it's cracked up to be. It's often just a sideshow.

After all, falling in love wasn't as nice as you were led to expect, and falling out of it has its compensations. Think of all the advantages. You can tot them up:

You'll have time to see your old friends again.

You won't have to hold your tummy in.

Your telephone bill will go down.

You can push away the cottage cheese and low fat yoghurt and treat yourself to a slice of Black Forest gateau instead.

You can go to bed at a reasonable hour with a cup of cocoa, and who cares if the cocoa trickles over your cold cream.

You can fall asleep to Radio 3 playing more baroque chewing gum and not to a snorer's Ninth Symphony.

You'll be less nervous, so won't break so much china.

And though sadder, you will be safer, for it's not prudent to hand so much power over yourself to another human being – only to God.

And also it isn't necessary. You don't need someone else to tell you you're worthwhile and lovable. You can do that yourself.

You don't need somebody else to find peace. The quietness is already inside you, if you decide to use it. How long is it since you sat back and prayed for it and not just presented God with a shopping list as if He were a department store?

Through prayer you might even begin to discover the seed of your next love in the death of the old. Your second affair might be with love itself. And that is a very deep truth though it comes from a juke box.

Ah, you will say, but if there's no person, what about sex? You can't have sex with love itself. Yes, it is difficult loving without sex if you are used to sex regularly. But, being realistic, not romantic, some sex is just habit, some of it is in your mind not your body and a lot of it isn't all it's cracked up to be. Sublimation isn't a dirty word. For example, I've been working so hard lately on cookery books, I haven't even had time to have a depression, and you can apply that to your sex life too.

Prayer and Black Forest gateau don't make for ecstasy at first, but in combination they can make you content,

and if you've been let down in love some quiet contentment is a great relief.

The old Jewish people I knew only aspired to contentment, for their lives were hard. If they were at death's
door, the kind Irish nurses at the London Hospital used
to ask 'Are you comfortable now, Mr Cohen?' and because they couldn't understand much English, and who
had ever worried about their comfort, they were puzzled
and said, 'Don't worry, I get a living nurse, I get along!'

He who hesitates

I have begun to realise that I must go away on a retreat
again. My religious instinct tells me it is time. What
surprises me always is the strength of my other instincts
which tell me to do no such thing.

Over the years I have learned to stand back from this
battle of the instincts and to watch the struggle appre-
ciatively with some detachment.

The anti-retreat voices begin with their objections,
which start off by being very high-minded. 'You have no
time for such things,' they say. 'Judaism is a religion of
this world and you must sit at your desk and over fulfil
your norm. Religion means serving society.'

I consider this but ask myself what it means in practice.
Sitting on more committees? Arranging more religious
divorces?

The anti-voice then continues: 'God is everywhere –
you know that there is no need to go to some God-
forsaken hole in rural England in December. You can
find Him (or Her) just as well with central heating at
home, can't you?' Of course, I know I can find God
everywhere but in practice I don't. I also find in prayer

that I have to take a step towards God, before He takes two steps towards me. Stepping into the unknown (even if it is a very safe and secure unknown) is the best way of invoking His presence. 'So,' the anti-voice continues, 'you insist on being so gentile. All this prayer and inner life, what is it but romantic subjectivity?' The inner life, I agree, hasn't been a feature of the Jewish life I've known, which has been a mixture of liturgy, communalism and committees. But I remember that the rabbis of old meditated for hours before their prayers and I think of the inner conversations in the Hebrew scriptures and I know that I am not the odd man out in Jewish tradition.

'Don't you think,' says the anti-voice, 'that counselling would be more scientific? You could do that better in London.' 'Well, yes,' I reply, 'knowledge of myself and knowledge of God have to go hand in hand or I shall become a fanatic or make God in my own image, but the former does not replace the latter. God is within me, but my ego does not limit Him (or Her).'

Listening to this inner argument, I wonder what it is I am afraid of, what I am avoiding. Is it that nothing will happen in prayer, or that something will happen? Either way causes complications. Religious experience isn't necessarily nice. It can mean facing yourself as you are. But emptiness can be worse. Perhaps I had better not put my religion to any sort of test. It might not be able to stand it.

But if I don't, what am I left with? The rat race, success and failure in worldly terms, and none of that great reserve of power and courage which has always helped me, wobbler though I am.

The anti-voice is not done yet, and now it gets to basics. 'You won't like it there,' it says. 'The heating will be sparse, and the tea too strong. The prayers will be too long and the food will be stodgy with too many calories, and you are already overweight. You won't get any smoked salmon where you are going.'

But my other voice also speaks. 'All this is trivial stuff. OK, you won't get smoked salmon, but you'll get things that matter. Some companionship in that part of religion where it really counts. The friendship of God is like any other. If you neglect a friendship and don't speak or meet for a long time, you get out of the habit, and the friend becomes a stranger. If God becomes a stranger it doesn't affect your public life, of course. You'll be able to gas on about religion and it might be quite popular. (People prefer synthetics.) But it will be gas, or like a cheque that has no money to back it, or like a public personality, or an empty conventional promise.'

The prospect of becoming a fraud to myself is more than I can bear. I pack up my little suitcase and slip in a detective story and a half-bottle of home-made wine. As I get towards the station, I feel that lightness which comes from not giving in.

A light touch

I wouldn't take life very heavy, dear, I wouldn't take life too heavy. You need a light touch with it. It's like making an omelette or learning to ride a bicycle or curing constipation – the more relaxed you are the easier it is.

Lots of problems get eased if you have a light touch. Take forms, for example. Don't fret if you can't fill in the answer to every question, and don't get defeated and push it away in a drawer. I used to think at one time that I should know the answer to everything – now I realise that you just have to learn to live with a lot of problems, not solve them. Anyway, the form might be wrong, not you. After all, it wasn't designed for you personally. Just fill it in as best you can and when you've got stuck, put it in an envelope with a little note saying that you've done your best.

But don't dither, get up and post it straight away. Don't let it hang around in your pocket (you know what happens then). As soon as it's in the box you'll get such a sense of relief.

And don't worry so much about prayer. As a child I used to make life hell for myself by inventing all sorts of little trip-ups, like not walking on the cracks between paving stones, or having to touch every third lamp-post. A lot of prayer and religious practice gets in the same compulsive muddle. I can tell you from experience that if you miss an occasional service or make a mistake in saying the office nothing is going to happen. God is not going to hit you with a thunderbolt, and if He did He wouldn't be worth praying to in the first place. Don't get frantic if you can't find a place of worship that's open. After all, God is everywhere, as you know.

If you can't find God, then just stop running, give Him a chance to do the work instead and let Him find you. If nothing has happened with all that kneework then relax in your chair with a cake and cuppa, stop forcing and wait and see what happens. It's possible God gets more pleasure if you are comfy not contorted when He speaks to you. After all, you are supposed to be fond of each other, you know.

'It's the real thing'

I was recently asked to choose a religious virtue like you choose a chocolate out of a box. The one I plumped for was not piety but generosity because without generosity of spirit I don't believe in any of the rest. If you go through all the right motions, alternately buttering up or bribing the Almighty, the result can seem very much like religion, but the test is generosity. It doesn't matter what formula you use in prayer – traditional or radical – the question is, do your prayers make you big or small, generous or mean? If they make you smaller or meaner, I suggest you look again at your brand of religion. Perhaps you should trade it in for another, for it's doing you no good.

There are many ways to pervert religion and the perversion of religion is a speciality of the affluent West. In the East it may be oppressed but it is worthwhile to examine our own ways of neutralising the religious message. The methods are so simple and innocent-looking that sometimes we do not see how deadly they are.

One trick goes like this. There is always a difficulty in speaking to God, because He (or She) is infinite and we are finite. Therefore the distance between us is so enormous that it seems impossible to bridge the gap. There are two ways round it. One is legitimate. Using this way we try to grow towards God, become bigger ourselves, more God-size. We try to be kinder, to have more patience, to do more than strict duty or even self-interest requires. In other words, we make ourselves more generous and more loving.

There is another way, which is not legitimate, and a cheat's way with religion. Using this way, we do not make ourselves bigger to bridge the gap but try to make God smaller instead. We do not try to change ourselves, because that is too demanding; we try to change the nature of religion, to distort it for our own purposes. God becomes the extension of our own prejudice. We deify our own limitations, and make our meanness cosmic.

This is a common device in all religious fanaticism, when nobody is willing to listen but everyone is willing to pronounce. It is easy on religious committees to get so absorbed by the small print that the great print of 'generosity' is lost. The small print, however clever it is, then only becomes the funeral rites of a real religion, which once lived.

I have met many 'religious' people in the course of my life. A very few were genuine saints, quite a few were phony, and most, including me, were a mixture of both. How did I distinguish the true from the false? Ideology isn't much use for such a basic question. The only testimonial I looked for was their generosity.

Eleven plus in prayer

'It must be lovely,' said the lady to me, 'being a man of prayer.'

'Lovely?' I answered. 'Well, yes, it is lovely, but it's jolly hard work too.'

'Hard work?' she asked, puzzled.

I tried to explain the set-up to her.

When you start off in prayer you often get a lovely lift off as a bonus that can carry you along for quite some time. But then the fizz fizzles out and everything is flatter than it was before. Then it's hard work, hanging on to a memory and hoping there is something at the end of the tunnel.

Lots of people give up at this point – they were only in it for the kicks. If you decide to carry on, then you now have to use your head as well as your heart. Thinking things out is a necessity and feelings dispensable luxuries. You no longer enjoy the pleasures of prayer, you have to puzzle out its problems instead.

One problem arises because prayer is, at least on the nursery slopes, rather fun and you can easily get addicted to it. It can turn into undemanding, moony cosiness. Thinking about someone sentimentally is not the same thing as praying for them – that is work. In a hedonistic society, after drink, drugs and sex the last and most sophisticated high in reach is mysticism. Since the aim of prayer is 'the abrogation of the ego' then it doesn't do any of you much good if you make your hedonism cosmic. The pleasure of prayer is a legitimate one and should be enjoyed when it comes, but you must not hang on to the pleasure alone or think God does not exist because you have not had your daily shot of ecstasy.

Another problem arises out of increasing progress and familiarity in prayer. There is a temptation to become smug and look down in a kindly, pitying way on your non-praying friends. You don't know what the point of their lives is, so only God can compare your spirituality with theirs. Anyway, in this area competition doesn't apply. Because of this feeling of superiority, people pray *at* each other, not *with* each other or *for* each other, and I have been at both ends of this rather nasty experience.

There are many things of which I am told I should be ashamed in life and am not. But this misuse of prayer for one-upmanship or aggression or spiritual pride is the thing I regret most deeply in my life. It is a blasphemy in a deep sense.

There is also a desire to flaunt prayer as a weapon in a holy war, to parade your traditionalism or your radicalism as a banner or flag to show off your membership of some group. Since the aim is to make your neighbour uncomfortable by making him feel an outsider, this is not prayer, even if the worshipper, so-called, is garlanded with objects of devotion like a Christmas tree. This was a problem for me when I was a rabbinical student because of my own insecurity and the burden of other people's expectations.

There is another problem with the love which comes out of the innerness of group prayer and we sometimes try to cheat our way through this problem rather than face it. We use prayers to increase our love for our own family, our own group, or our own religion, by withdrawing love from everyone else. This seems to increase love at the beginning, but at the price of mortgaging future religious growth.

All of us come to religion and to prayer with the wrong questions and the wrong demands. The trouble arises if we stay with them, after we have learned better. There is no harm in asking 'God give me this', or 'God give me that', provided you know you might not get it, and approach it with the same humour as Topol in the song 'If I were a Rich Man'. All that we know for certain that God can give us is Himself. He will also let us find Him, we are told, if we seek Him in the dark places of our life and He will come and live with us. But do we want Him inside us? At a certain point in our prayer life, the consequences of prayer sharpen dramatically. It is no longer a pleasure, it is a demand for internal change. As in any other relationship, we have to ask ourselves if we want to go on and venture out of our depth. It is only when we are out of our depth and stumble, leaning on God who doesn't seem to be there, that we pass our eleven plus in religion.

It can be painful working through all this. But there is a great prize at the end. You will have really earned your right to whatever ecstasies you get. Your religion may be less dramatic than it was before all this probing started, but it has one great advantage – it's your own. You worked for it, the hard way, and no new theology, or ideology, can ever take it away from you.

But how do you say all this to an unknown lady, when a sherry is balanced in one hand and a piece of tinned asparagus in the other. 'Hard work,' I repeated firmly, and she moved away rather miffed.

Absurdities

Religion is heady stuff, and to prevent yourself getting
inflated like a hot-air balloon, you need to keep a firm
hold on common sense. The tension between religion
and reality provides paradoxes for theologians and
absurdities for rank-and-file believers.

While we are saying grand things about redemption in
our prayers, one part of our mind runs after the recent
rises in rates. Also because the difference between God
and people is so great, prayer can be comic, though not
silly. The comparison of religious claims to religious
practice may not produce cynicism but will produce
hilarity.

On a deeper level, the absurdities of the human situation, and the jokes which reflect them, should be pon-
dered (though not too heavily), for among the ecclesiastical formalities they insert a sort of Western Zen –
deflating, disconcerting, but honest.

The cost of coffins

I was chatting with an elderly nun I know about the cost of coffins. It was really rather grim, she said, how everything was going up, and it was very inconvenient. She had slept in a coffin for years, a modest one though specially made for her, and though she could not say her coffin was comfortable or cosy – indeed it was not meant to be – she had to admit it fitted her well enough both physically and spiritually, and was really quite snug.

But to her surprise she had outworn her coffin, and as it had to be custom built on the Continent, for the shoulders had to fit, a replacement was out of the

'Do you do part ex?'

question. A new one was dearer than a repro four poster fitted with concealed amplifiers. Her mother superior had exclaimed that holy poverty was out. It was too expensive and they would all have to resign themselves to comfort on a divan base like everyone else – if you could buy them without mattresses.

I sympathised with her on the loss of her coffin because in a similar way I had become very attached to a shroud which I took with me on all my travels, and had recently mislaid. I had put it for safe keeping in a plastic bag and left it behind on a bar stool in Frankfurt Airport, so I cannot speculate on its fate.

It was a natty number in white cotton which my aunt ran up for me as a wedding present when I was wobbling towards matrimony. It had a festive look for she had sewn folds of artificial lace round the neck and cuffs. Even when I wobbled in the other direction, and had to send back most of the wedding presents, I kept my shroud – it was not the sort of thing you could 'return to sender'.

Like many Jewish people I wear a shroud on some important festivals, such as the Day of Atonement, and eventually I hope to be buried in one. From the point of view of fashion a shroud is not a success. I shall meet my maker looking like a piece of meat, a chop adorned with white frills, the kind you see in high-class butcher shops. A colleague told me brusquely that Aunty's shroud made me look like Gilda in the second act of *Rigoletto*, when she is fleeing from the Duke in a white nightie.

But its whiteness still recalls the purity from which I came and to which I shall return. Like Sister's coffin it tells me that to enjoy the life of this world I should not clutch at it, for the world is not as solid as it looks, just as my shroud is not as silly as it seems. In fact, neither coffin nor shroud is ornamental but fundamental – because they can help you to live truly. If you know, for example, that an eternity awaits you, you stop being so greedy and can afford to enjoy the taste of the world a little more, for it is very like chocolate. If you suck it slowly you get the flavour – if you gobble it, you just get indigestion.

This greed comes from insecurity and a feeling that the world will cheat you, which it must do if it is the only world and you treat it in this way. Only a sign of mortality can give you enough perspective on life to enjoy it. Some friends of mine leave a little corner of their living room unplastered, to remember that though their detached house is cosy with central heating, it is not their eternal home. Such knowledge prevents much pain.

But perhaps you're reading this at breakfast, propped against the teapot. 'Why Fred,' I can hear you say, 'that rabbi's rabbiting on about coffins. It does make me feel queasy and queer so early in the morning. I should have read the newspaper instead. Pass me another kipper, dear, and that napkin. Yes, Fred, that one with the lace edging, just like the rabbi's . . . Oh dear!'

'*Look at that rabbi in the window*'

The voice over the telephone was sweet and deferential, but in it I detected a hint of steel. Would I be kind enough to sit in the front of a department store and sign copies of a book I'd written?

I inclined my head slightly towards the telephone like minor royalty and graciously agreed to spend an hour signing books for whoever wanted . . . 'If they want, of course,' said the voice at the other end, 'ha, ha . . .'. 'Ha, ha,' I echoed tremulously.

As soon as I put the telephone down, I panicked. What would happen if nobody did want? Would they confiscate my pen in public? Would I be ushered from the shop? I could see them counting the pile of books, averting their eyes and shaking their heads.

But say people did come up for books and I had no pen, or I had one and the ink ran out. Or perhaps they would say, 'Rabbi, write something in it which is short, witty and profound' and the pen wouldn't dry up but I would.

That is how I came to sit in a department-store window, flanked by dummies who looked down on me. Being nervous I had arrived early and they were my only company. Have you ever inspected the dummies in your High Street window? Perhaps you'd better not if you lack confidence. They are snooty creatures, who sneer at you and each other, high-bred hussies for whom Hampstead and Highgate are as Hoxton and all they care to seek out is Sloane Square through slit snob eyes.

I panicked again. What would passers-by think of me? They would think I was like one of the ladies who sit in windows in Amsterdam knitting away in plunging négligés. But surely they wouldn't. I was, after all, the wrong sex and the wrong shape. (The dummies snickered.)

A Jewish lady pressed her nose against the glass and then shook her head slowly and silently. I felt forlorn, and needed mother love and chicken soup. For one wild moment I thought of crashing through the glass and putting my arms around her, muttering, 'Momma, Momma!'

But she probably couldn't make chicken soup. She probably bought it already canned. She would just pass on to me the names of her children – her daughter the shrink or her son the psycho, whose services alas, were not obtainable on the National Health.

I thought of the last bunch of letters I had received.

66

With one or two exceptions they were so helpful and encouraging. But the exceptions!

One gentleman (anonymous) had accused me of leading Pakistanis to the Potteries – though why he never explained. Another lady (signature illegible) informed me I had brought tears to my dear old mother's eyes. This letter had incensed my mother greatly, for she had just bought a natty new twin set, and did not see herself as a Yiddisher Mother Courage. The only tears she admitted rose up from rage after being outflanked at a Harrods sale.

All my Englishness started to slip away and I began to sink back into the great Slav gloom of my childhood.

Could I ever do anything right, I wondered? Would I always fall off pulpits and into graves? Would nobody ever love me, except God of course, who had to, and therefore didn't count? Would somebody ever buy a book and rescue me from those damned dummies?

And as I prayed the nice lady from the publishers came in with a cuppa. I was in the wrong window, she said, and had got mixed up with remnants and ends of lines. In another window a little queue had formed who were waiting for my name. Bouncy with relief, I told her I would do more. I would write an inscription in their books – something short, witty and profound, I thought.

Oh Lord, what do you make of us with our pride and paranoia? Do you delight in the dottiness of your creation? I suppose You take us with a pinch of salt – You certainly created enough of it.

Marrow with a message

When I wake up I hate listening to the news – there is so much sour anger around. It's justified anger of course, so they tell us, but it has a rancid taste and it stops me jumping out of bed. I pull my duvet back over my head instead.

And wherever you go the scenario is the same dreary stuff, whether it's in Lebanon, Northern Ireland, Yorkshire or India. One side clenches its teeth and shouts 'wogga, wogga, wogga' and then the other side snarls back 'wagga, wagga, wagga' and then after a few bleats and baas from the high-minded both sides settle down to a bottle session – throwing them unfortunately, not drinking from them. And with the bottles they throw all these dear old tribal bygones, hurled since time immemorial: bricks and bottles to warm things up, followed by the hard stuff – bullets and bombs.

To get some relief, I switch off the radio and start brooding over my own domestic problem, which at the moment happens to be an enormous intractable marrow left over from the harvest festivals. The trouble is I don't need a marrow; I need a message with a moral which I can turn into a sermon. There should be a message in my marrow, because it was grown in a monastery and given to me by a monk, but it eludes me and this makes me angry – though not enough to throw a bottle.

It is a very big marrow and a very firm one – so firm in fact that none of us at home can cut or stuff it. We stabbed it with carving knives and sawed it with bread knives, and have drawn blood – our own – while the bloody marrow (I speak factually, not pejoratively) sits secure and smug in its skin.

But I have a clever friend called Pauline who finally took it on, because she makes models and sculpts, and she intends to bore a hole in it and throw out the pips. Then she is going to fill the hole, she says, with dark brown sugar and a pinch of ginger and punch another hole in its bottom and then hang it up in an old pair of tights – washed of course. The fermented marrow juice or liqueur will then drip through her tights into a suitable bottle, and one day we shall get merry on marrow, she says.

I am not recommending this recipe. I can merely describe it as I just do not know what will happen, for another monk assured me that in his monastery a marrow exploded when it was treated in this way. They kept on renewing the sugar, he said, but you can have too much renewal. The smell of their marrow was so strong it blotted out the odour of their sanctity.

Now I suppose there are some moral messages I can squeeze out of the marrow, though they are not as exciting as its juice.

I could say that from sweetness is distilled the liquor of life. I could also say that if you don't treat God's creation with respect it will blow up in your face. But, neither of these turns me on, and I can't deduce anything from a pair of washed tights.

But I've got the glimmering of an idea about how to use an exploding marrow. It could be just the job for demonstrations. It wouldn't be lethal like bullets, or as dull as old bricks, and when people saw it flying through the air in a pair of tights they might learn to laugh again and recover their humanity.

I think that's what people need now: not another rehash of anger, whatever theology or ideology it's packaged in, but something new, something unexpected like an exploding marrow – something fresh which comes as a nice surprise, like the manna which dropped from heaven in the wilderness or a strange star that rose in the east.

A holiday from myself

I don't think I'll be able to have a proper holiday this year; I'll only be able to have bits of holiday as opportunities arise.

But this morning I gave myself a lovely bit: I decided I was going to give myself a holiday from myself. For one whole morning I wouldn't let myself be bullied by that voice within me which makes me feel guilty about everything I do and mucks me up.

You know the sort of thing. Just as you are about to crash into a slice of toast and marmalade (with marge, not even butter) that awful inner voice starts to go on and on about duty and charity, and though you eat the toast because it would be wasteful and useless not to, the voice takes the joy out of the marmalade and puts the guilt on to the gingerbread.

I'm also going to give myself a holiday from horrors. Yes, I might have leprosy, housemaid's knee, piles and the plague and don't know it, but until 12.45 p.m. I'm not even going to think of it. And that goes for the Bomb as well. I shan't protest or demonstrate until I've had the longest soak in the fullest bath, foaming with a few pennorth of 'orchid' detergent I splashed out on at the supermarket.

I am also not going to dress, but wander round the house in my oldest, most threadbare and comfortable bathrobe, which I didn't even buy but inherited. (It came from Harrods in 1936.) And if anyone knocks, who cares! They'll have to lose their ecclesiastical illusions. After all, religion isn't a dry-cleaned suit with deodorant and dentures. I don't know what the prophets looked like, but I suspect they were kitted out in old bathrobes like me and never used after-shave, if they ever shaved at all. (What would they have used – flint?)

I'm also going to enjoy some religion – yes, I mean enjoy it! I am going to lie on the floor and listen to the lush bits of *Elijah* on the gramophone, with plummy voices backed up by lashings of strings and brass. I don't care if my inner voice agonises as to whether it is kitsch or culture. I enjoy it in a damp sort of way, because the vibrato turns on my tearducts. In the sad parts I shall allow myself to moan with the horns.

I am not going to be persuaded into thinking about my prospects – and that includes pension (if any), wardened flats, retirement homes, and jolly geriatric trips to the seaside (out of season). I shall read adverts for hair replacement instead, which – hair! hair! – always makes

'And thirdly I'd like another three wishes.'

me think more hopefully and happily about our moans and hormones.

I shall read comforting religious thoughts in homey magazines and look through D I Y journals to find out how to make a bedsitter 'regency' at minimal cost.

I shall do all the things my inner voice disapproves of. I shall chat on the telephone, while sitting in the bath. I shall eat cold custard straight from the tin (not sitting in the bath). I shall plan dinner parties I'll never give. I shall concentrate on my favourite childhood game: 'If a witch gave you three wishes what would you wish . . .?'

I shall pray, not standing upright nor kneeling nor prostrating, but comfy and civilised in a cushioned chair with a glass of port.

Until 12.45 p.m. I am going to love myself as my neighbour. I shall keep eleven commandments, not just ten – I shall not commit myself!

I am contemplating my navel and cannot be disturbed.

The case of the bearded bride

I once went to a monastery at Christmas. Word came down from above that we should 'rejoice', and being an obedient lot we tried very hard to be light and spontaneous. We spoke at table, we clinked glasses and toasted each other in thick, sweet, tonic wine. We laboriously told jokes, though we were so anxious to draw the line that we lost the point. It was great – we all said so.

It was a relief next day to get back to the penitential life, to listen in cosy, gloomy silence to the sayings of superior saints, and to extinguish the awful aftertaste of that wine with strong stewed tea. At last we were able to feel glum again, which is a reasonable response to life, and an old monk told me in private that he was tearful with joy now that the party was over and he could meet God again.

In this he was mistaken, for since God is everywhere when you go to a party He goes too, the divine gate-crasher.

The rabbis of old knew quite well that the Almighty was interested in parties. When I was a student for the ministry, prodded on by my teacher, I brooded for weeks over the following rabbinic problem. At Jewish weddings it is customary, indeed it is obligatory, to go up to the groom and tell him what a lovely bride he's got. Now, say your best friend invited you to his wedding, and just as you were about to tell him what a lucky chap he was and what a beautiful bride he had, you peeked and suddenly realised she had a beard. What can you say in all honesty about a bearded bride?

The rabbis agonised over this and one of them thought he had found the way out. She might, he said, look somewhat queer in the eyes of man, but perhaps she was a pious woman and beautiful in the sight of God. So, therefore, there was no problem. Go up to your friend and slap him on the back and say, 'Old boy,' or whatever the equivalent is in ancient Aramaic, 'what a beautiful bride you've got.'

But the rabbis of old were not cowards. Unlike more modern clerics they preferred to face a problem head on. So they insisted on asking the awkward question: what if she has no spiritual beauty either, what if she is not only bearded but loose? So what do you say to your friend if you go to the party and find he has just married a hirsute harlot?

Now this is a serious matter. Do you spoil the party or tell a white lie? In all my studies this is the only instance I have found when the rabbis were prepared to relax the rules of strict honesty. To save the party and spare the newly married couple and everyone else a social disaster, they gritted their teeth and said, 'You go up to your friend with his hairy love beside him, and without batting an eyelid you tell him what a lovely bride he has got – and God help you if you snigger.'

I used to be amused by this problem but it is important to remember that God is not only present in poverty and penitence, in sacraments and on altars. We can experience Him when we are off duty. Sometimes at a party, for example, you are holding a glass of sherry in one hand and a bit of asparagus in the other and you are gabbling away like mad. And while you are doing this, one bit of you is somewhere near the ceiling, watching yourself dispassionately with the eye of eternity. Isn't that a religious experience?

So chin chin, amen, your health and halleluyah!

My own funeral

This is my advice to fellow anxiety sufferers, who wrote to me asking what I do about it. Well, when there are disputes and strife around me my anxiety increases. I then make a list of all the things I have ever worried about and put a tick against those which have actually happened. I can't tick one item. Then I make a list of all the nasty things which have happened and I find I have never worried about any of them. So the only thing I have to worry about are things I don't worry about – and that itself is very, very worrying.

Like a lot of people, when life gets too tough I retreat into harmless fantasy. Since people were brave enough to tell me theirs and asked me to come clean about my

74

own, here it is – and I admit it with embarrassment.

What I do is mastermind the arrangements for my own demise and subsequent funeral. It's my self-pity scenario or 'Heroism through Tears'.

In my fantasy, when I'm told I've had it, I smile through my tears and forgive everybody who has done me wrong. Since this includes all my friends and relations it gives me a chance to pay off old scores in the sweetest manner imaginable. What rotters they will feel when they know!

The funeral will be without ostentation, though it is my secret hope that the cortège will be both numerous and glamorous. But even in fantasy some reality steals in, so I hurriedly arrange a posthumous whisky and smoked salmon wake to encourage the reluctant.

Of course, I want to be laid unostentatiously but reverentially in a sweet little nook off the beaten track, but with reasonable communications, of course. Some cute little corner in the stockbroker belt would suit me fine.

I sat in an empty synagogue on my way to work thinking about all this. As my eyes filled with tears at my own fortitude and generosity, it seemed to me that the Almighty was cackling his head off. When He had stopped laughing and wiping his eyes so to speak, He began to plant his thoughts in my mind.

'Firstly,' He said, 'I really advise you against being a peeping Tom at your own funeral. You know, Lionel, as well as I do – well, not quite as well as I do – what human nature is like. And there's going to be less sighing and more sniggers than you care to think.'

'In any case,' He added, 'it is all quite pointless because you can't be there when you are not there. Also,' He said, 'I've got a bone to pick with you, because underneath all that schmaltz there's an awful lot of aggression and spitefulness, you know.'

75

'I see he brought a bottle.'

   I did know of course, so I was a bit sulky and showed it. But the Lord gave me a hug, as it were, and when you know you are loved, and that's real, not fantasy, then you can laugh with the world and at yourself.

   Anyway, no flowers or condolences yet.

Other Faiths

I was brought up in a closed society but I live in an open one. Sometimes, like many Jews, I get nostalgic for the society I left, but I have to admit to myself that if I were offered a return ticket I would refuse it without regret. I do not want to un-know what I have got to know – that way lies banality or fanaticism.

I have got to know that God lives in traditions other than my own, and though my own is home to me, God is not limited to it. Quaker meetings, Catholic monks, and Hindu swamis have had their place in my religious education, and I could not and would not disown them. They helped me to become a rabbi.

There is a lot of one-upmanship in every religious grouping. It is there in me too, but I try to be free of it. It is a blasphemy to project my limitations on to God and make the cosmos parish-size.

One lost soul. Finder rewarded

There was a knock at the door, and a neatly dressed gentleman presented himself. Politely, he asked me if I had lost my soul. He had a leaflet which would help me locate it.

It was such a personal question, I bridled. It was like asking a stranger if he had bad breath. But his question hit me, so I answered equally politely. No, I hadn't lost my soul exactly, because it's a tough old soul which bounces back like rubber, but I had mislaid it among all the committee meetings I attend, just as I mislay my credit cards and my railway tickets.

Though my answer left him restive, I thanked him and said goodbye, for I decided on the spot that I was going on a retreat. I rang up a monastery I knew which had provided me before with good quality silence and started to pack my bag. There was my bathrobe, slippers, half a pair of pyjamas, prayer book, pre-shave, after-shave and splash-on.

It never used to be like that, of course. Twenty years ago a stick of deodorant caused much comment and was considered 'worldly', which is a monastic term for 'sissy'.

At that time we slept on boards. It was so cold in winter that I needed to pack very little. My toilet was simple or non-existent. When I went to bed I took off my shoes, said my prayers, and bounded on to the boards, overcoat and all. Getting up was equally simple. I put on my shoes, cleaned my teeth, and risked a lick of water, if it hadn't frozen. I then trotted off to the chapel, lured by those incense smells, which are like holy Turkish Delight. I was a bit sore about the middle because of those boards. Whenever I turned over at night, I got speared on my hip bones.

In the chapel we must have smelt a bit gamey, like venison, as it would have been foolhardy to brave a bath. Cleanliness might be next to Godliness, but you can't have it all. The retreat master must have thought that icy moorland was a good antidote to passion, and in this he was more accurate than Emily Brontë. Up there in winter I don't think I gave a thought to sex, even though I was younger and friskier – and that was not because I was holy, just frozen.

Real prayer is hard work and makes you very hungry, and I must have looked like a gorilla as I tucked into great wodges of bread (marmalade like deodorant was 'worldly') and tea so thick with tannin it looked like oil.

When I went back to visit my monastery again, it wasn't like that any more. The cells had that bright, chintzy look, just right for middle-aged, middle-class clerics with a bulge around their middle. The incense had gone too. Instead, I smelt a fellow retreatant's aftershave, and we clashed something awful.

You may well ask why someone like me traipses off to a place like that, for temperamentally I am more suited to Costa Packet (three stars, HB, PB and balcony with supplement). I ask myself the same question, because a lot of their liturgy I can't say and don't believe, apart from the psalms of course, and I get edgy whenever Jews are mentioned in the readings. Also all institutional smells put me off, and the incense doesn't drown the fish and the furniture polish.

I go because holiness is so rare. I've found it among some contemplatives near Marble Arch, sitting with a Hindu teacher on Euston Station, and with my monks doing the washing-up. As my grandpa said, 'When a horse drops from heaven, don't examine its teeth.'

St Peter's wife?

A few weeks ago I went to a study weekend for Christians and Jews, and I've just recovered enough from it to be able to pray again, because it left me so confused and cross.

Prodded by the Christian leader, reluctantly I spelt out all the problems I have with the gospels. Nervously I came out with all the questions I don't think one is supposed to ask. What happened to Peter's wife when Jesus called him? He had a mother-in-law, the text says, so therefore he must have had a wife – and what did she think about it when he went off? And who were Jesus's sisters, and how could he have had sisters? And what does it mean when he says 'let the dead bury their dead' because that's left to the living – I know because I've just been to a meeting working out the politics and finances of a burial society. And how did the Holy Family function – it isn't like any family they tell you about in marriage guidance.

I was quite angry because all this was forced out of me, and I was nervous about the results. I remembered nostalgically those nice, safe, Jewish-Christian meetings when we sat together in prayerful silence, or sang, 'We shall overcome' though what we were supposed to overcome I never figured out – each other perhaps, though no one dared say so.

I was helped by a story told by a Jewish therapist. It's not a Christian story or a Jewish one, but a Muslim one from Iran, which says a lot. I later found out that the best version of the story is told by Idris Shah, whose works I recommend.

Nasruddin saw his neighbour on all fours scratching about in the dust outside his house. 'What are you doing?' he asked.

'I've lost my key, and am looking for it,' said the neighbour.

'Well,' said Nasruddin, 'two heads are better than one, and four hands are better than two. I'll come and help you.'

So both started searching away outside the house on all fours. But they couldn't find the missing key.

'Are you sure,' asked Nasruddin, 'that you lost the key outside your house?'

'Well,' said the neighbour, 'actually I lost it inside the house.'

'Then why are you scrambling about for it out here?' said the puzzled Nasruddin.

'Oh,' said the neighbour, 'it's so dark inside the house, and there is so much more light out here.'

I got the point. You need courage to face confusion, and trust to cope with darkness. If you want to find the key to understand another religion you have to be prepared to shake up and be shaken. Christians and Jews never really meet unless they have the faith to speak out on the Holocaust, the Crucifixion, and the bad experience they have had of each other over the centuries. Evasion gives the illusion of meeting, not its reality. And this story does not apply only to religion. You need the same courage really to know another person and especially to know yourself and your own darkness.

We had a reward for our painful honesty. We were able to tell each other things which are normally kept inside the family and tell religious jokes which were not for export. I haven't enough courage to tell the jokes the Christians told me, but here is an inner Jewish one I told them.

A saintly rabbi went up to heaven and was given a great welcome. 'The feast stored up for the righteous,' they said, 'is awaiting you.'

'That's nice,' he said, 'but who supervises the dietary laws up here?'

'But surely,' they said, 'you can rely on us, for this is heaven.'

The rabbi stood his ground politely: 'But who supervises the dietary laws up here?'

'Well,' they said, 'the Holy One, blessed be He, supervises the food laws.'

'Hm,' he said, 'in that case, I'll risk a little fruit.'

Some of the Jews remained in the dark and never got the key to the story. But one old nun cackled away, and hasn't stopped laughing since.

Religion is a problem

'What are you going to talk about on Monday, dear?' said my mother, peering over her paper at breakfast.

'I've got around three and a half minutes to speak about religion, one world, the United Nations and world peace,' I told her.

'But Lionel, you can't', she said, and she looked serious. 'Just look at these papers, dear. Look at Northern Ireland and the Middle East and India. How can religion solve their problems when religion is the problem!'

I couldn't contradict her. She was right, or almost. Religion isn't all the problem, just a big bit of it, and it's not right to tell pious fibs or pretend to protect God from the truth when really you're only protecting yourself.

Over the years which I've spent at committee meetings I've asked myself, What is a religious organisation? Well, it isn't paradise and its members aren't the communion of saints. Religion is a messy, untidy place where we try to join together two realities which don't fit easily and never will – this world and kingdom come, your prayer life and your sex life, retreats and rosaries with the rates bill, your see-through soul with the sauce and the sausages you had for breakfast. My father was a tailor who stitched different cloths together. I try to stitch different worlds together, but I'll never be as successful. After all, how would you run an organisation when you ought to give all you have to the poor? How do you chair meetings when everyone has to do what is right and follow his conscience, yet all be bound by a majority vote? After a life-time as a minister you've impressed a few adolescents or some people who are vulnerable because they're in hospital or in love. What sort of a business is that?

That's why we are tempted to cut corners and take refuge in politics or tribalism, but we don't succeed in making them pious – they just make us nasty.

What saves us, I think, is that we know the problems aren't outside us but inside us, not just in others but in ourselves, so we can't turn our enemies into devils very easily, and also because we are told that the Truth we serve is not partial. It is beyond all parties and all prejudice.

Even when they were in conflict the rabbis granted that the new Christian sects were as full of good works as eggs are full of meat. And Mother Julian, the medieval mystic in Norwich, remarked when she visited hell that it was completely empty, there wasn't even a Jew there!

And I am grateful, for it was very broad-minded of her at that time.

You can learn the lesson in religious jokes. A minister goes to heaven and is introduced to the inmates. Behind a high wall he hears the sound of hymns. 'Who are they?' he asks. 'Sh,' they tell him, 'don't speak so loud. That lot believe they're the only ones here, and we don't like to disturb them.'

But you and I are not like that. We know we worship the same God. You just pray to Him in your way, and I'll pray to Him in His.

An exclusive ghetto

On holiday in Ibiza you could mix with two sorts of people. In the museums there are some very disting-uished dead. Hannibal was born there, and there are lots of encrusted Carthaginians. To judge from their re-mains, they enjoyed a rather suburban life style, not unlike that in Ilford or Wimbledon today, but with some bad habits such as human sacrifice. On the other hand, you could mix with all the youngsters pouring in from northern Europe, set to have themselves a ball. They were pink, peeling and patchy, and the museum lot warned me against the disco lot. They were riddled, they said, with drink, drugs, divorce or even worse, and I should keep away. But they were much more fun to look at than the mummies – and so much more lively. So I ditched the departed and dived into a disco and when I had recovered my hearing I watched with interest.

There they were shuffling away in their frillies and briefs, in their panties and undies. Some of them danced on tables but as both were quite sturdy no one came to any harm. Occasionally in the flashing light they grimaced at each other, because speaking sweet nothings was useless in all that heavy metal. I found the noise nostalgic because it reminded me of the ack-ack and air raid sirens in the Battle of Britain.

I never saw anyone drunk the whole time I was there. I never saw a single fight, and none of the phones was vandalised. One young man did admit to owning a hypodermic but he had left it at home in the kitchen drawer.

Why there? Well, its use was legitimate, though bizarre. He had a girlfriend back home who liked her grub. Give her Chicken Kiev and she was away. He couldn't afford to butter her up, so he marged her instead, and like me, she couldn't tell the difference. He filled his needle with melted margarine and injected it under the bird's thigh skin in cheap chicken joints. It worked admirably he said, and you could put on the style, even on his pay. It certainly pleased her and I pass the tip on to you, because learning has no frontiers.

One of the youngsters asked me if I had been to a disco before. Many many years ago, I told him. When I was young and on a lecture tour, an elderly theologian had invited me to a drink in a night club, which also called itself a college of striptease. He dropped in there occasionally, he told me, because it was the only college in the area which had never awarded him an honorary doctorate.

Later on in my holiday, I sat in the local church to get some quiet, while some elderly ladies in black shawls whispered their prayers. It was a sad situation. The reality was in one place, but the religion was in another, and they never met. Did priests or pastors ever have a drink with the youngsters, or chat to them at their tables (when the music stopped of course, otherwise confessionals would need amplifiers)? I hadn't realised until I went to the disco what a small ghetto we ministers lived in. This is a pity because young people are very vulnerable and suffer from heartbreak at that age and need a lot of kindness. They needed the consolations of religion (which are real) but they were locked away, and no one knew how to find the key.

Conversations

The first words of the Hebrew liturgy are quotations from a conversation recorded in Genesis between the prophet Balaam and his ass. The ass was wiser and more pious than the prophet and God used him.

I, too, hear the voice of God in some chance conversations. He doesn't speak the words but He seems to speak through those of other people. Often a chance remark reveals a dazzling truth or a darkness I had never grasped before.

The insights of religion do not always come to us through formal sermons in formal services. I myself am too armoured and protected against them. They come instead when I am undefended because I expect them least – in waiting rooms, in hospitals, in the departure lounge of an airport, on a bench in a crowded railway station.

Preparation for purgatory

We were the last flight in the departure lounge at the airport, and the voice over the Tannoy spoke as the last judgement, the voice of doom. I had always imagined the voice of doom as bass, but it was soprano, and as the news got worse it got higher and higher until it disappeared into an indignant upper-class squeak. 'We regret your flight has been delayed' – and then it almost slipped off the scale – 'indefinitely.'

The consternation was frightful. People pleaded with the officials, with each other, and then with God, but the former could not and the latter would not change the pattern of the universe to suit their convenience. Then followed a choice conversation which I still think over many times.

In the confusion a small, elderly lady sat perusing the *Church Times* while officials hurried past us, averting their eyes.

'Young man,' she said severely. I felt flattered. 'Why don't they look us in the eye?'

'Because they think our misfortune is catching,' I told her. 'That's why people don't visit friends in hospitals. They send postcards instead, so that the bad luck won't rub off on them. Superstition is so much more natural than religion.'

'That is a most interesting observation,' she said and eyed me keenly. 'Are you of the cloth?'

'Yes,' I replied, pointing to the *Church Times*, 'but my cloth is made of the wrong material. I'm a rabbi.'

'Then why do you travel to Berlin?' she enquired.

'I'm going to an important religious conference,' I said proudly, 'to give a lecture on sex.'

'Good,' she said. 'Then this delay is of no importance to you. I was in Berlin both before Hitler and after, and I can assure you that there is little for them in Berlin to learn on that score. They've been at it for years. But please help me find the airport chapel and join me in Compline.'

'I will certainly join you in the psalms,' I said, 'but surely God is the same everywhere and this departure lounge is a good enough place to worship.'

'Young man,' she said severely, 'certainly God is the same everywhere, that is well known, but I am not and I need a chapel.'

The arrows with a Muslim crescent led to a door that was tightly bolted against believers and non-believers alike. The Stars of David led through a service door to two overflowing dustbins, but the crosses led us to a chic, gaudy chapelette. Our feet sank into scarlet carpets, cocktail lighting played on textured walls, and scattered around were little purple poufs for petitions and prayers.

'Most unsuitable,' she said. 'To whom is such a place dedicated, I wonder?'

'Rahab,' I suggested.

'Hm . . .' she responded and we returned to our seats in the departure lounge.

'Human nature is so piteous,' she commented, 'so buoyed up by foolish hopes.'

And sure enough, a lady sitting nearby was saying she had heard from a reporter who had got it from an engineer 'that our engine was only stuck in forward drive, that's all'.

'Poor creature, does she think we will fly backwards to

Berlin? Undignified and impossible. Human hope is so piteous.'

And a man was demanding his rights. Apparently we were all entitled to a four-course meal in a three-star hotel.

'Foolish people.' She shook her head. 'We assign ourselves so many rights but how can they be encashed? Yet this delay affords us time to prepare ourselves for purgatory, to which hopefully we are all travelling. Have you any thoughts on time young man?'

'It is relative,' I said.

'Poppycock. Illustrate your proposition.'

'Well, an old rabbi asked his grandson, a young scientist, to explain the relativity theory of Professor Einstein. The boy said kindly to his grandfather, "It's like this. If a gorgeous blonde sits on your lap, the hours pass like seconds, and if you sit on a needle, the seconds seem like hours."'

'And what did the old rabbi say?' she said suspiciously.

'He thought it over and said, "Son, from this, Professor Einstein gets a living?"'

Before she could comment, our delayed flight was announced on the Tannoy and people pushed towards the departure gate. She folded her paper saying, 'They could have flown to heaven but they missed that flight.'

The blessing of baked beans

The bus was very crowded, so I concentrated on an article in my newspaper about pork pies. An eminent gourmet living in England, but with the right French connections, had stood up for the pork pies you can buy on British Rail. The meat was moist, he said, and the pastry succulent – or perhaps it was the other way round because, as you realise, I am in no position to confirm or deny it.

But it's good that someone on high has spoken up for our grub and we don't have to feel guilty any more if we don't order those expensive spinach leaves soused in raspberry vinegar but shepherd's pie instead.

Lots of beautiful people have low tastes in food. A lady, renowned for her intimate dinners, told me she always carries a 'B bag', when she is invited to an important houseparty on the Riviera. The 'B' stands for basics – bronzing lotion, Bible and a bottle of British brown sauce. She hides the bag among her Gucci and Pucci with her missal, for though fashionable she is also devout.

The bus I was on was a bad-tempered bus. A group of noisy youngsters had collared most of the seats and people were having to stand. My neighbour and I had each earmarked and fought for the inch of seat between us. He had won but in revenge I angled my newspaper so he could only read about the sinking pound and not about the high-rise pies. I relented though, ashamed, when one of the children got up to give his seat to a lady. The boy was pink with embarrassment and so astounded at his virtue that it made me smile.

My neighbour smiled too, and as we got talking he told me he was into baked beans. He was proud of his job and I listened sympathetically as he carefully set out the protein in his product and its goodness. I told him that I was partial to them too, because they were therapeutic. This interested him for he had not heard of this angle before. I explained that if I woke at an impossible time like 4.20 a.m., I headed for the larder and was comforted by a tin of baked beans, eaten cold from the tin with a teaspoon. I had tried them with Worcester sauce and salt and pepper, but now I preferred my beans classical. If I wanted to put on the style I ate them with a silver spoon.

He complimented me on my taste and asked what business I was in and what was my product. After a moment's hesitation I told him I was in the God business and dealt in salvation. He chewed this over and said he preferred baked beans. They seemed more certain.

He touched me on a sore point for an old lady in my community had bluntly asked me whether, if she were religious, she would have a better chance of getting to heaven. How could I be less exact with my product than my friend was with baked beans?

While I was brooding over my reply all the children started giving up their seats because virtue is infectious and the self-satisfaction that goes with it was a new experience for them.

Looking at them I knew how to answer the old lady. Religion will get you to heaven if that is where you want to go. But heaven isn't an object like a tin of baked beans and you will have to consider what you will get out of it and what is the taste of its rewards. Well, the rabbis said the reward of one good deed is another good deed, just as the consequence of wickedness is more wickedness. So if you like goodness for its own sake then heaven is for you. If you don't and feel cheated by this, you had better do some hard thinking as to what you do want. Heaven isn't a time or a place, like an appointment or a bus stop. It's something already inside you. So it isn't necessary to strain for it, you discover it or stumble into it like the children in the bus.

My grandfather told me of a man who wanted to see heaven very much, and his wish was granted. When he got there he saw the sages poring over their scriptures.

'Why,' he said, disappointed, 'it's no different from what they would be doing on earth.'

And God said, 'You've got it the wrong way round.

Don't you realise the sages are not in heaven. Heaven is in the sages.'

The bus halted suddenly at my stop. I shot out and tripped over a trolley and heaven disappeared as quickly as it came. My product is more certain than a tin of baked beans – it just doesn't seem as solid.

The waiting game

I sat in the waiting room of the hospital feeling annoyed and sorry for myself. A fat lady pushed on to the bench beside me. I forced a polite smile and moved up. 'Well, ladies,' she exclaimed to the others on the bench, 'it can't be me looks, so it must be me charm.' She then burst into a peal of laughter and dug me in the ribs. I reddened with embarrassment and envied all those people who 'went private' and could read *Country Life* in high-class hush in the expensive gloom of Harley Street.

She then brought out a brown paper bag and poked into it. Like a conjurer producing rabbits from a hat, she brought out first a corned-beef sandwich and then a broken Eccles cake. She considered both carefully, and then dropped half the Eccles cake into my lap. 'Eat it up, duckie,' she said, 'and it will sweeten you up.'

She was quite right, it's no use fighting the system, it's better to relax into it. I bit into the cake and asked her how she could look so happy. 'Well,' she said, 'it's me weekly treat coming up here, and if you bring your own grub it ain't expensive.' She told me how if you only had your old age pension you had to make up your treats – even out of the weekly visit to the hospital, and though the canteen food there was cheap, it was not cheap enough for her – so she brought her own.

96

I should like to thank her for showing me how to transform a torment into a treat and I pass on these tips to fellow middle-aged sufferers, whose plumbing is starting to seize up and who share the problems of their own secondhand cars awaiting the MOT.

If you are not on a diet, now is the time for comfort eating. A bag of home-baked biscuits is a good investment. If the bottom is about to drop out of your world, my advice is nibble and it will help you to endure the shock. Yes, I know there may be 113 kilo-calories per cookie, but a cookie takes a lot of weight off your mind. Also, if you pass them round, you become popular with your fellow pensioners, and a good deed which benefits you in this life as well as the next is as good an investment as a Telecom share.

If your ailments are respectable, then talk about them. If they're not, and you've got the nerve, you can still talk about them – the world of the waiting room is inquisitive but not judgmental. But if you talk about them, sauce up your symptoms to make them interesting. Curse if you

97

have to, people will only turn up their hearing aids, but don't whine. It is anti-social to undermine people when they need a little courage and laughter.

Keep your eye on your file and notes and watch where they go. If they get lost, you fall into a crack in the NHS system – a black hole – and you become a non-person. Though it's not your fault, you begin to feel guilty for existing and a nervous 'pardon me for living' whine creeps into your voice. 'Yes, nurse, I handed it in, I really did . . . I really am a patient of Dr So-and-so. Yes, I'm sure I am. I've been seeing him for years. No, I swear there was a file . . .'

In the waiting room time has no meaning. The hours pass and seasons change, you've seen them come and you've seen them go. So, take a nice thick book with you. *From Here to Eternity* sounds right and passion is pleasant if you can munch a cookie when you get to the exciting bits. But why not try the Bible in a modern translation? It's big enough and it is not as respectable as you think. There's quite a lot of guts and gore, and some juicy passages in Kings and Chronicles, which the nicer sermons never reach.

Cooking my way to heaven

I met an elegant old lady at a party. She was handsomely dressed and wore her clothes with distinction. Just as we were getting into conversation a waitress put a plate of smoked salmon sandwiches beside us, and I went to the bar to get us two dry sherries. As we resumed our chat, I reached to the plate for a sandwich, but they'd all gone, not a crumb left, and I wondered indignantly who could have wolfed them in so short a time.

She stared at me for a moment and then said, 'When I was in a concentration camp I learned to eat anything I could when I could. Excuse me, but I can't break the compulsion. You only know the blessing of food when you don't have it.'

I asked the waitress to get us another plate, reserved two portions of blessing for myself, and looked away as she handed the plate to my friend who devoured the rest as quickly and furtively as she had the first plateful.

There were some people in the camps, she said, who gave away their own ration of bread and starved themselves. There were others who ate each other. 'Food, Rabbi Blue, is the gate to heaven, and the gate to hell.'

Going home on the last underground train, I thought about what she said, though concentrating on the heroism not the horror in her story.

Food has always been one of my gates to heaven. Indeed, when I think of heaven, I think of restaurants. What comes to mind are the Lyons Corner Houses in all their grandeur which dotted the West End before the war.

We used to queue up to get into them on Saturday nights after the Sabbath ended. As we stood on the stairs, we could hear the tinkling music of the little orchestras, playing selections from *The Merry Widow* or *No No, Nanette*. And when the doors opened we glimpsed glittering lights and real marble pictures of castles and waterfalls. You really felt proud when you were allowed in and ate your egg on toast under those chandeliers.

Your entrances and your exits were controlled by a doorman in a greatcoat, sparkling with gilt epaulettes. Like St Peter he decided whether you spent another weary hour in the passage-way purgatory or made it into the genteel paradise. Eventually, all of us did get in, and I hope it will be the same with heaven, though of course we shall probably have to wait a bit, for you never get what you want at once in this world or the next.

We got to know a lovely waitress in the Coventry Street Corner House at Piccadilly and used to manoeuvre in the queue to find a place at her table. It is easy to terrorise people who are unsure of themselves and being both Jewish and poor we were sensitive to slights. One remark about our clothes or religion could wreck the treat so carefully planned, so often discussed, and in the thirties such remarks were common. Anti-Semitism was still fashionable, only just about to become vulgar and then horrific.

She treated us like lords. When we commented on the chandeliers she just said, 'You paid for 'em, ma'am,' and reassured Pa, for he was too shy to ask, that there was no pig in the pie.

I last saw her in August 1939. When I went back to the Corner House at the end of the war the windows were boarded up and sandbagged. The orchestra had been replaced by an electric organ which played the 'Jealousy' tango as you ate carrots and turnips, in the ingenious combinations recommended by Lord Woolton.

I looked for her but the Nippies had gone and she had vanished with her tribe. But she had taught me a religious lesson I have never forgotten – serving food with generosity (not just because you're paid for it) is a way to heaven, whether it's in a concentration camp or at a party, a Jewish Kiddush or a Christian communion, or just waitress service at Coventry Street Corner House.

A trivial incident

If you're wise you will realise that jokes are not always joking matters and that God can reveal His hand at a cocktail party as well as on a mountain top.

I'm going to tell you about a joke I heard at a party and the commentary on it the party provided, which I've thought about a lot, though it was really quite a trivial incident.

Three of us were standing together near the tit-bits. I had gravitated towards another clergyman for clerics huddle together for mutual protection at parties. Lots of people don't know how to treat ministers. Some go on and on about the state of their souls, and they feed you with little scraps of Jung or such. And you have to look a bit surprised and soulful and say, 'Yes, yes, it's too, too divine' or something equally ambiguous.

The other lot feel compelled to prove that you've got feet of clay, as if you didn't know it. So they tell you smutty stories, and you're trapped. If you laugh you're smutty too, and if you don't, you're impolite. In my case, you've heard them before – told much better by your colleagues.

With us was a lady who had joined us, I suppose, because she wasn't paired off. She was in good form, though I knew she had had a rough time. Anyway, she was sympathetic and brought out the best in us. I told a harmless joke from the Old Testament, and the Christian minister capped it with one from the New. It's not a disrespectful one, so I can repeat it, and in any case I had already heard a Jewish version of it about a saintly rabbi.

It was about the incident in the gospels concerning the

woman who came to Jesus possessed by seven devils. Just as he was about to heal her and expel her devils, she whispered urgently, 'Master, may I have a word with you, may I make a special request?'

'Of course,' he said, 'tell me.'

'Can I tell it to you very privately?' she added.

'Of course,' he said again, and bent down putting his ear close to her mouth.

She whispered into it softly, 'Only six, please.'

We laughed and exclaimed how terrible it would be if we lost our devils all at once. Who would ever invite us to parties again?

The lady left us to chat to an old acquaintance, a man, who had just arrived. He was also in good form and the lady began to sparkle as her appearance was admired and her wit appreciated, and I was pleased for her.

Later on, I glanced up. Another woman had joined them, and I was puzzled because the lady had fallen silent. She was listening quietly, just putting in an occasional remark. It was the newcomer who had begun to do the talking. I supposed she had put my friend's nose out of joint so I went over to comfort her.

But she saw through my artless manoeuvre immediately and said in an amused way that she wasn't yet ready for the consolations of the clergy. 'If you're a single woman,' she said, 'and you get on well with an attractive man, you always sense the first faint whiff of adultery in the air. As soon as his wife came over I knew I had to help her, let her shine and take a back seat myself.

'I've been thinking, Rabbi, about that joke we heard, you know that one about the bit of devilry the woman kept back. A bit of devilry is OK provided you realise it's not a tabby cat you're playing with but a tiger. That's how I lost my husband.'

'Good day, gentlemen. Nice meeting you. I did enjoy your jokes.'

Places

Europe is dotted with places of pilgrimage. Travel agents, the railways and souvenir manufacturers provide different blends of piety and package holiday to satisfy all tastes. I do not sniff at such things. God may be the same everywhere, but I am not, and it is easier for me to discern His kingdom in some places than in others.

As well as public shrines we all have our private ones – a house we once lived in, a restaurant where we fell in love, an old cinema or theatre, so glamorous once but now demoted to bingo or boarded up.

To compose the scripture of our lives we must meditate at such shrines. So I do not head for Jerusalem or Lourdes but buy a ticket to Whitechapel or Oxford Street instead. My mind, possessed by the past, begins to work out the message I couldn't figure out long ago, but now I just barely begin to understand.

Holiday blues

Apart from the Bible, of course, and Shakespeare, my favourite reading is holiday brochures. Like you, I am already collecting the new summer ones – they're free and fun and I never tire of blue skies and hotel balconies with their explicit promise of sun, and their implicit suggestion of sex. Each year the magic works, and I

prepare to get packaged on a costa, waiting for my fish and chips and vino, and ready to belt out *Y Viva España* with the best of them.

I am fond of the smiling couriers with comforting names like Julia or Juliet or Jenny or something, who deftly and kindly put us in our places on the coach at the airport.

'And this is your real Spanish driver. His name is José, and he would like you to say hello to him.'

And we all sheepishly mutter 'Hello, Hosey', and are gratified when he growls back in real Spanish 'Allo!'

I like the cut and thrust as I prise my way to the buffet. It reminds me of war and I get sentimental and hum that ill-fated melody, 'We're gonna hang out the washing on the Siegfried line'.

Over the years, I've learned from experience and pass on these tips to you.

If you have a beard like mine, avoid the paper fresheners they give you on the aeroplane. With the stubble, they make you kind of fluffy, and who wants to dance with a middle-aged Jewish Santa Claus amid the plonk and passion of a Majorca disco?

Also never forget you're British even in foreign parts. Slip some digestives in your denims and some yeast extract in your you-know-what. Wrap a bottle of brown condiment in your pyjamas and panties for 'though trendies shout, and gourmets sneer, we'll keep our butties saucy here'.

Another thing you should take with you is your own happiness. Although it may seem from the pictures in the brochure that it comes automatically, if you consider the small print you will know it can't. You'll get comfort, of course, and I admit I would sooner be unhappy in the Ritz than in a boarding house. But I have also been very happy in a boarding house and unhappy in luxury – I can't speak about being unhappy in the Ritz because I've

106

never had the opportunity, though I wouldn't mind a try, as a spiritual exercise, of course.

Anyway, happiness isn't an object, it's a state of mind. You can't buy it, so you have to create it. And how do you create it? Simple! Make someone else happy instead!

That's why I would pack a religious book with the sun oil. I'm not suggesting a complete edition of the Talmud or the Church Fathers because they are weighty in every way, and you don't want to pay excess baggage and let your spirits sink like sterling.

For sometimes among all the plastic and the instant paella and the disposable passion, you notice the face of a tired hotel cleaner, or a lonely person in the lounge, and you know that even with the fun deep down you're a bit tired and alone as well, then you long for something which isn't instant or plastic or disposable. You get a craving for a holy day, not just a holiday, for the real McCoy in fact, and that is just another name for God.

It happens in Ireland

One of the nice things about going to Ireland is that things happen, and I don't mean bombs, battles and other macho bygones. In the old days, before Common Market subsidies made Erin the land of milk and money and the whole place got a face-lift, you never knew what was going to happen next. The money has ebbed away of course, as money always does, but you can see the ranch houses, Texas style, peeping out of the turf, and snob suburban gnomes have replaced the sadder saints in front gardens.

When you got off the boat, they didn't search you for booze or after-shave. They weren't interested in your body, or indeed anybody, only in cattle and God. The customs officers warned me against foot and mouth disease and gravely examined my books. But my tastes were too low to give offence, for only the very best in modern Irish literature was forbidden. I was gratified by their interest, as until then nobody had shown much concern for my soul and its welfare, and I felt flattered.

I wandered into a little 'snug' in Wicklow in winter, and was even more flattered. I was the only foreigner there, and the lady behind the bar asked me what I did. I confessed to being a student rabbi and was startled and pleased when she bobbed at me saying, 'Holy mother, sure our house is honoured!' I nearly fell off my stool, but I had enough manners to mumble 'thank you' and when the other customers slapped me on the back I peered into my Guinness and blushed. It was before Vatican II but they were already a jump ahead of it.

In Connemara, there was another happening because the roof fell in as we were having supper and a swag of plaster flowers fell into my soup. In England the meal would have been continued with awful solemnity, the plaster, which was the *pièce de résistance*, not passing anyone's lips, either for conversation or digestion. On the Continent there would have been fulsome apologies right up to our departure. In Ireland the offending plaster was passed from hand to hand and admired. 'Sure 't was a nice roof, and we'll never see its like again!'

I also happened on a nice monastery with a church attached. The monastery was painted mauve and acid yellow, and the brothers patched up my bicycle, and me too, for they plied me with Paddy and prayer. Afterwards they showed me round the church, which was the last word in scientific modernism. It was very smart, for instead of flickering candles there were banks of electric bulbs. You put in sixpence and a bulb lit up for hours. I have a fondness for slot machines and religion so the combination appealed to me hugely.

There has been news of yet another happening in the Republic – a serious one this time, and a supernatural one. It is said a statue of the Madonna has moved. Now many clerics and theologians of the modern sort get affronted and say that such things don't happen, or if they do happen they shouldn't happen, or if they happen to happen they don't signify.

I have never witnessed a wonder myself, but friends of mine, whom I respect, have told me of such things in India, and there are many strange stories about the pious rabbis of Poland in my great-grandparents' time. Cures

'I'm not sure a rebate from the Inland Revenue counts as a wonder.'

at Lourdes are well attested, and no one has ever explained away Fatima.

I wonder what would happen if I too witnessed a wonder. If one happened to me, it would signify. I make no bones about it. What it would signify I'm not sure, but I don't think I'd ever be the same after as before.

A church crawl

Lots of people go on pub crawls. I don't join them because while they get jollicose and then bellicose, I just get comatose and fall asleep. I haven't the head for such things, and to be honest prefer a milky drink, a duvet and a banana as oblivion descends.

But I do like church crawls or synagogue crawls, and I'm especially attracted to the ones in side streets, known only to the experts. During my career I've seen them all and done them all. There was a lively synagogue in America, where the pulpit rose up in the air electronically, just as I was about to give the sermon, leaving me like a monkey on a stick. I clung precariously to the railings, addressing somewhat nervously the human blobs below. There was another, where the lights turned blue as I got to the memorial prayers. A delicate touch? Mmm – you have to be wary of high tech pulpits.

Some places of worship I've tripped over, or into, have come to mean a lot and I drop in whenever I'm in the neighbourhood. There's a synagogue near Marble Arch which is lovely, but my prayers go best in a quiet little room just above it, set aside for worship. It's very simple and rather bare, but it never feels empty. Whenever I'm there my inner conversation starts up.

Also near Marble Arch is the Tyburn Shrine. As the

buses and lorries are thundering round the Arch, you only have to open a door and you are suddenly bathed in the loveliest, most luminous silence. It's like a pearl, and as I sit in it, before fighting my way home in the bus queue, I feel laundered inside, light and clean. It was a wonderful tonic when I lived in Bayswater. The Sisters, whose church it is, also never minded about my dog. She was a pious animal who stood up and sat down when the congregation did, but she was also a sniffer who got high on incense.

Once, on the way home from Broadcasting House, I came across a church near the Middlesex Hospital. It was like a garden with so many flowers, and a lady smiled and moved an electric heater next to me because my pew was cold. I was also given a free lunch (you could make your contributions in a box). Good bread, two types of cheese, Eccles cakes and instant coffee. It was served with dollops of generosity, and God bless the people who served it, because you don't often find the fresh milk of human kindness these days, only the canned sort. This will do, of course, but it's not the same. By the way, I recommend the hospital chapel itself for a good pray. The decoration's a bit heavy, but you get down to business fast.

Occasionally people ask me (or I ask myself), what are places of worship for? Over the years I've puzzled on this. Do they just provide another tranquilliser, like alcohol, or Valium? I don't think so. I see them as factories – not producing steel or plastic or computers, but increasing our stock of generosity and decency. When Europe started its journey to hell in the early thirties it didn't happen just because there was a crisis in consumer goods. There was also a shortage of spiritual goodies too. There just wasn't enough niceness to go round. Now where is goodness produced? In the churches, synagogues and temples of Europe, I suppose.

But they are not efficient, and few people use them, and sometimes as I sit in them I can't help shivering – but not with cold.

Kosher in Ireland

I was in the kitchen eating tinned pilchards with a can of Coke when the telephone rang.

Would I care to go to Ireland, savour its gourmet cooking and write a judicious report about it?

'Ireland,' said the voice, 'has made remarkable strides in delicacy.'

'It was no longer just a pig in a pan?'

'Oh no, no, no . . .' the voice laughed intimately, 'No, it's all lightness and schnitzels and elegance now, to be sure – no longer liver and lights.'

I quickly put my newspaper over the pilchards, lest vulgar vibes from that poor fish should filter through the phone. I bowed my head towards the receiver and spake (it was that sort of occasion).

'Hmm,' I said hesitantly, and licked my lips, 'it might be possible. One' (get that for style) 'might be persuaded at this time of the year. Mightn't one?' I wiped some tomato sauce from my mouth.

The telephone rang off with expressions of mutual esteem, and 'one' took the newspaper off the pilchards, added more vinegar, and washed it down with a swig from the can. I was bloody angry with myself. After all, you never know who is going to ring, and you should always be at your best, toying with a slice of smoked salmon, a copy of *War and Peace* propped up against a champagne bottle. And if you have to cover up your tracks with a newspaper, let it be the *Osservatore Romano* or the *Financial Times*, or the *Standard* – something chic with class and style.

I sat back and thought smugly about my rise in the

world. On my first visit to Ireland, many years ago, I had consumed my first Irish delicacies on a boat limping through a gale towards Dublin. My salt-beef sandwiches were sodden with salt-water and dribbles of Guinness. I shared them with a squad of black nuns, and we were all sick over the same rail. We were very ecumenical in spirit, for they cried out 'Mother of God!' in chorus and I replied involuntarily 'Holy Moses!' They smiled approvingly at me, and then we had to rush once more to the rail.

I experienced another delight of Irish cooking in a monastery mainly inhabited by Irish monks. On Saturday nights, the novices put the week's left-overs in a pan and sprinkled curry powder and home-made ale over it, and let it cook itself overnight in a slow cooker. The main ingredients were porridge, piety and parsnips, and after a week of tiring knee work in their chapel it was delicious.

I enjoyed it, but would 'one' enjoy it? Was it good enough for a gourmet or a gourmand, if one knew the difference.

I told one to go and stuff himself, because an aspect of things occurred to me which had not hit me before. Covering the pilchards once again with the paper, I telephoned the voice.

'You know,' I said, 'I'm a rabbi, ha, ha.'

'Ha, ha,' echoed the voice obediently.

'And rabbis are Jews, ha, ha,' I continued with remorseless Thomist logic.

'Ha, ha!' repeated the voice.

'And Jews don't eat prawns – Dublin Bay or otherwise – oysters, ham, hocks, bacon or Stroganoff.'

'Ha,' said the voice uncertainly, which I interpreted whimsically as an Erse '*oy vay*'. 'What do you rabbis live on then?'

'Cheese, and Guinness, and fish . . .'

'Oh, fish, that's fine, what sort of fish?'

'All sorts. Anything decent, you know,' I replied, 'Halibut, salmon, sole . . .' and I turned my head away, distancing myself from my pilchards.

'Sure, you'll be welcome, you're coming now?'

'Sure, sure,' I said, 'one will be honoured,' and I shamelessly hid the tin opener in a drawer.

Latin lovers at Studio One

I was a youngster, and the war had just ended. I had queued up at Studio One to see my first French films, and felt very sophisticated as I hummed '*La Vie en Rose*' (I couldn't sing it because I had only done six months' school French and the words were beyond me).

On the last day of term I took my rucksack to school, and as soon as lessons ended I headed for the open road, to hitch-hike my way via Newhaven and Dieppe to romance, garlic and Gauloises.

Paris was a disaster. It started off with a colossal row, the cause of which baffled me completely at the time. When I arrived there, I took a seat on the terrasse of a café, and commanded the waiter with nonchalance and *savoir-faire* to bring me a glass of Evian and a glass of water. Eventually he brought me the water, and I with great politeness forbore to reprimand him, though I was longing to let myself go on the lush sophistication of Evian which I had never tasted, but which had been mentioned in a glum and gloomy Continental movie. Eventually my patience broke. This was my first time in Paris and I wanted to drink my full of decadence, to the dregs if need be. Courteously but nervously I demanded my Evian.

A curious conversation then took place, in which all the people from the neighbouring tables got involved. It eventually became quite a fracas, and though what little French I had soon evaporated, I filed away curious words and phrases, which I knew would never be of use in School Certificate examinations.

The focal point of the fracas was the glass of water which had been palmed off on me. I laboriously tried to explain that I would surely overlook this, if I could get at the Evian. This reasonable suggestion raised tempers to fever pitch, and I was ejected, steadfastly refusing to pay the water bill. This *petite histoire* was charming and chic, but unnerving, and I burst into tears as I walked away from the Gare St Lazare along the Boulevard Haussman.

What made it worse was seeing so much jollity in the cafés. I felt like a hungry child looking into a baker's shop, separated by plate glass from all the delights. There they were, I thought, having causeries (whatever they were), lovers to a man or whatever, and the women all mistresses. And when they weren't making love, they would be humming 'La Vie en Rose' (with the words) and jabbering away about existentialism and Sartre. How I envied them!

In London it didn't matter if you were perplexed and pimply because everyone looked sad in London. But in Paris they all looked as if they were having a really good time, and this made my own gloom much worse.

So I left Paris in disgrace and hitch-hiked south, there got ill, and was taken in by some kindly friars who inhabited a great rambling ruined priory in the foothills of the Alps. Some of the brothers wanted to learn English. I had with me a copy of *Finnegan's Wake* by James Joyce, which I had bought in Paris, to suit my new sophistication. In fractured French, and trat Italian, I taught them English syntax from that remarkable novel. They were grateful but confused.

116

In return they cleared up my own confusion. I learnt that Evian was water, and I hung my head. Soothingly they told me it was very high-class water, special water, even without bubbles, and I shouldn't take it too hard.

They listened gravely to the words I had noted in the fracas and shook their heads. They advised me against their use.

They pointed out that when the Cardinal Archbishop of Paris had opened a new church, a workman on the site had hit his own hand with a mallet and had exclaimed, '*Nom de Dieu*'. This the good Archbishop had overheard, and had admonished the workman gently. '*Mon fils*,' he said, 'don't blaspheme. Say *merde* like everybody else!'

Hearing this I hung my head, because I was so gauche, and there was so much baffling sophistication to mug up.

I thought of all this as I walked down Oxford Street the other day and saw they were pulling down Studio One. I felt as moody as any of the sullen lovers stalking through the French films I had seen there so many years ago.

Professionalism

I am a religious bureaucrat with a desk, chair and diary and an office filled with files. I hover anxiously over my files as I keep them moving from the 'in' to the 'out' tray.

Years ago I would have despised such work, and said it was not creative or mystical or spontaneous. Indeed, it is not any of these, it is just necessary, and makes the world go round. It is not spiritual cake, just ecclesiastical bread and butter, but godly all the same.

God is present as I answer a telephone or wade through a heap of documents. I can do either with care and compassion, or uncaringly and unkindly. The same choices exist for a bureaucrat as they do for a contemplative.

I have also realised that the function of religion is to marry together the reality of this world and the reality of the next, and be faithful to both.

Problems for professionals

The Jewish New Year is approaching, and I am trying to think about my sins. When I first became a rabbi many years ago I knew quite well what they were. As I've got on in life I've become less certain. God has a way of using everything I've got. Sometimes, to my annoyance, He ignores my virtues, such as they are, and prefers to work through my weaknesses.

What do you make of this for example? As a minister of religion you have your highs and your lows. Sometimes I'm in love with God, and His presence feels very close. Sometimes He has just vanished, and it feels like I am trying to peer at Him through the wrong end of a telescope. Sometimes I am so fed up, I can't even be bothered to try.

What do you do if you are a minister in that situation? I can't shut the shop, close the synagogue and put a little notice outside the door saying that the service this morning is cancelled because Rabbi Blue is suffering from an attack of doubt. Whether you like it or not the service has to go on, though it doesn't seem more than a show.

It once happened to me like that and I decided I would just have to get through the liturgy as best I could. The congregation had arrived and I had to give them something. I used every bit of technique I possessed, though I was in a very depressed state. I modulated my voice to fit the words, mechanically but quite effectively. I whispered some, I declaimed others. I surprised myself unpleasantly by putting a throb in my voice. I wooed the congregation with synthetic sincerity, and they said afterwards that I was a doll.

I felt awful, and went to one of my teachers and told him what a dreadful thing I had done. All I wanted was to be told off and get defrocked or something. I could hardly believe my ears when he said to me that it was probably the best service I had ever taken.

Was he taking the micky out of me? I looked at him suspiciously. After a pause, in a businesslike way he told me why. 'When you took that service,' he said, 'you weren't thinking of yourself and what you were going to get out of it, spiritually or any other way. You only thought of your congregation and their needs, not of your own. At last you tried to do something for them, without bothering about little spiritual shivers going up and down your spine.'

I sat back confused. Then I asked him another question. 'What is religion?' I said. His answer surprised me, and I have never stopped thinking about it. Here it is and you can ponder it too. It's a strange answer. 'Religion,' he said, 'is the art of giving freely without strings.'

In the intricate web of life you never know what part of you God is going to use or what purpose He is going to use it for.

Take the case of the saintly teacher who had a saintly disciple. When the teacher died his disciple took his place. And in due course the disciple died too.

When he got to heaven they asked him gently what he desired. 'If only,' he said, 'I could see my saintly teacher again.'

Well, a door opened, and there was his saintly teacher, and a beautiful girl was bouncing up and down on his knee.

'Oh, my teacher,' he said. 'Is she your reward for all your saintliness?'

'No,' said the teacher gently. 'She's not my appointed reward. I'm just her appointed punishment.'

'Don't take it too heavy, dear, don't take it too heavy.'

Teach yourself religion

The eminent social worker introduced himself to me at the meeting, and I had a feeling I'd seen him before. He was amused at my fumbling and mentioned a nickname I don't care to remember.

Good Lord, he was the boy I had taught in religion classes when I was studying to be a minister. I used to watch him plotting in the back row, and I couldn't sleep for rage when I thought of him. It's bad enough being persecuted by Gentiles but when Jewish children join in the act – it's tough.

I had been demoted from adults to children because it was felt with them I would do less damage. Because of my mysticism, you see. I had tried to say a service with devotion, milking every word of meaning, but it had gone on so long, everybody's lunch got burnt.

I explained to my children the categories of sin. There were big ones and small ones. 'Give me an example of a weeny one,' I said brightly. A hand shot up and my social worker answered proudly, 'Frowing a brick frew a window.' After that I struck 'sin' off the syllabus. The detailed confessions in the liturgy were too hot for my delinquents.

I retreated instead to safer subjects. I asked them in my 'let's all be bunnies' voice, 'What would you like to be when you grow up?' A nice little girl explained excitedly to her chums that she wanted to be a cantor's widow. She knew one who had a tin of iced cakes, and whose TV was never disturbed by a male brute. Her mother had said so to her father.

I tried to tell them about goodness, about loving little animals, honouring Mummy and Daddy, passing plates at parties and giving up your seat to your elders. They listened with brassy contempt and I kept them quiet by bribing them with chocolate if they learnt long psalms.

One day the chocolate ran out, and I broke down. I was incompetent, I told them tearfully, and could never teach them again. Like Chicago gangsters who wept over Shirley Temple, they were a sentimental lot, and I had moved their little bowels of compassion. From then on they treated me well in a patronising way.

'I suppose you didn't get much out of those lessons?' I asked the social worker. 'Not really,' he said. 'But you were a lesson yourself. It's because of you I became a social worker. You gave me my first feeling for deprived creatures.'

I think the only person whom I changed through my lessons was me. Although at the time I thought religion was a mystical experience, I began to convince myself of what I taught the children. Religion is standing up for other people and being nice to weaker people and passing plates at parties.

I learned another thing too – not to be a religious snob. God didn't bother to use my strengths, my little hoard of learning or my mystical flights, to get through to the children. He preferred to use my weakness. And weakness can be very strong.

It was announced in a Jewish village in Poland that the first Jewish trapeze artist was going to jump from a high wire into a barrel of water. Before he jumped, the lights went down in the crowded tent and the Yiddisher daredevil in sequined drawers addressed the crowd below. 'Look,' he said, 'don't you recognise me? I'm your old friend Issy. We played together as children. You know my wife Becky. Such a gentle kind woman, who is always doing a good turn. She loves me and I love her. And remember our children, so well behaved. Your own children play with them, and we give them all tea together.

'Now, do you really want me to jump?'

'Everybody's got one sermon in them'

The most terrifying sermon ever given to my congregation was also the shortest, and the least professional. It came about in this way. A friend of mine was an artist. It was his birthday and I asked him what I could do to help him celebrate. I was taken aback by his answer.

'Let me give a sermon from a real pulpit. There's a

good sermon in everyone, and I'd like to get mine off my chest.'

'All right,' I said warily, 'but don't make it too long or say anything improper.'

He assured me on both counts and I booked him in as a guest minister for a youth service.

When the day came he certainly looked ministerial in his borrowed robes, and because he was a novelty the young people were quiet.

I now give his sermon verbatim – the grave tone you can supply yourself.

'Children,' he said. 'Look first to your right, and then to the left. On one side sits your mother, and on the other side your father. Have no illusion, that is how you will be when you are grown up – the same, perhaps no worse, certainly no better. Amen.'

That was it. The young people were shattered. It was what they had always feared. For weeks afterwards they came to see me singly or in pairs. Would that be how they would end up? Surely life would be different for them?

Alas, I couldn't confirm or deny it, but only make encouraging noises. They drowned their sorrows in Coke, with salted peanuts. It was tough but that's life.

My friend had scored bull's eye and he was lucky, because most sermons never penetrate at all.

One of my students told me he was going to give a fearless sermon in an old age home. Nobody would talk to him afterwards, he said, with a martyr's gleam in his eye, because he was going to give it to them straight, the truth and nothing but the truth. Never mind about rejection, it was his duty to them under God.

What was the terrible truth he was going to unveil? I asked. Gossip, he said, and malicious tittle-tattle which was rife in the home in question. I wished him luck, and waited with curiosity for the results of this juvenile Jeremiah.

Well, he gave the hurtful sermon, and lashed them with his tongue, showing no mercy despite their age. It went very well, or seemed to, because you could have heard a pin drop.

When the service was over the congregation clustered around to congratulate him on his fearlessness. 'Like a lion,' they said. Everyone wanted to have a private word with him.

'What did they say?' I asked. My student looked drawn!

'Oh,' he said bitterly, 'everyone came to me and whispered in my ear, "Wonderful sermon, young man" and then they winked and said, "and I know exactly who you were referring to – no names of course".'

I soothed him and told him that preachers of truth were not appreciated properly these days. Perhaps he could concentrate next time on rarer sins for the aged, such as fraud or fornication.

But it is true, everybody has at least one good sermon in them. Even if people have never read a verse from the Bible, they still have the key to one scripture which only they can interpret – the scripture of their own life.

Three problems of professionals

1. *Lower truths*

I have been a religious bureaucrat for some years now. I see my religion from a desk and not from a pulpit – though that has not always been the case. I like my work, and I do not despise religious administration. God's will is done quite surely as the files pile up, and the same possibilities occur on the telephone as on a pastoral visit – the possibilities of generosity or rejection, the easy bureaucratic 'no' which prevents further questions, or the difficult but doubtful 'yes' which opens a Pandora's box of further questions and is a bureaucrat's nightmare.

These are the things which worry me in religious organisation. Though I am a Jewish rabbi of the reformed type, these problems affect all religious organisations in the Western world.

I often feel we are asking the wrong questions. We ask 'is it traditional?' or 'is it expedient?', 'will it be safe?' or 'will it cause a scandal?' They are not unworthy questions, but they are secondary ones. The first ones must be 'is it true?', 'is it real?' It is nice if the truth isn't a scandal, but you can't have everything.

Now truth is a tricky item, though all religion is, of course, committed to it. You can find it on one level and lose it on another. I think religion spends much time pursuing it on the higher slopes of prayer and contemplation, but it often loses truth on the lower slopes of common honesty and fact. In other words, for the glory of God and the most beautiful motives it is tempted to evade, and even to cheat. Now no good comes of being virtuous on the heights and a 'flibbertigibbet' in the depths. Religions are no different from people in that respect, and sooner or later that way leads to trouble.

The telephone rings on my desk. An uncertain, self-justifying voice says, 'Rabbi, may I have a word with you – now don't get me wrong!' Can we both face the truth or shall we rush for cover? I wonder!

2. Whole-some

One of the greatest problems of modern life is how things are split, and how un-whole-some we all are.

I sit in my little office and I deal with the forms that people fill in. I do not often see the flesh those people inhabit, and between the form and the flesh, dialogue is not encouraged.

I meet the people who can give spirituality, and the people who can receive it, but the former live in a religious ghetto, and the latter don't, and there is no transport in or out.

I think of all the spiritual conversations I've had in bars, cafés, and discos, and the financial ones I've had in churches and synagogues. I've watched ministers and laymen change place so smoothly that it's like a conjuring trick.

I've met religious leaders who have taken a strong stand against gay rights but have never met a gay person. I've met gay people who have passed resolutions on abortion, though for a lot of them it's none of their business.

The split is in me too. At unexpected moments it grows from a split to an abyss. I try to be devout in prayer but my mind is wayward and embarrassing. I come away from a retreat radiating light, and then quarrel with everyone at home.

For me religion does not mean taking strong stands, or being a little Festival of Light all on my own. It means learning from living and piecing together all the fragments of truth which God has scattered in my path. Before I become holy, I need to become whole.

3. Home truths

It is not easy to keep to the truth. I find it difficult because giving pleasure is so much easier. It is much less wearing to be liked than to be respected.

The temptation to sin against the truth came from quarters I never expected. Once I was safely locked in a religious organisation I thought all temptation would cease. How naïve I was!

When I was a theological student I tried to be obliging.

I gave the sermons which were expected of me and was pleased but oddly unsatisfied when my congregation told me how nice they were.

I had a sermon on Jewish family life. It was quite touching and in it I described Jewish family life as it might have been over fifty years ago, seen through a golden haze. I wasn't describing the inconsistent living present, which was dangerous, but *Fiddler-on-the-Roof* country, which was safer. It owed more to *Little Women* by Louisa M. Alcott than to any Jewish family I knew. It was a very nice sermon and quite false.

Many years later I was asked to speak on an interfaith panel – the usual combination of Catholic, Protestant and Jew. A colleague who was organising it came up to me. 'There'll be a question about intermarriage,' he said. 'You'll give them the old stuff,' he added, 'about how it never works and all that.' Now perhaps it shouldn't work, and perhaps it doesn't always work, but I have to admit work occasionally it does, even without benefit of clergy. I knew some intermarried couples, and their lives were no disaster. I managed not to tell an outright lie on that platform, but only just.

In Jerusalem, I was told, Arab and Jewish youngsters are attracted to each other and meet together in cafés and discos. I was expected to deplore such contact, but part of me kept silent. It seemed to me that in a town of religious resentments, and unholy divisions, this was an instinctive attempt to redress the balance, though not favoured by tradition. When the supernatural channels get blocked, God can work through the natural ones He created.

It's awfully difficult holding tight to the truth you know, your truth, the one you experience. It's a bumpy ride but worth it.

A dog collar at a party

It you wear a dog collar at a party there are dangers on two fronts. The obvious danger comes from those who want to do you down because they identify you with the Spanish inquisition, but you also have a problem with supporters who want to build you up. So just as you've filled your plate nicely with all the little bits you would never make for yourself, and have retired to a corner like a dog with a bone and are raising a fork to your lips, your digestion is shattered. A lady who has materialised from nowhere whispers hoarsely into your ear, 'Rabbi' (or Father or Vicar) 'you must help me – I'm desperate.'

Well, she is obviously in trouble so you put down your fork. 'I just can't sleep,' she wails, 'I wake up and think of the Bishop of Durham.'

You ponder for a moment and then in quick succession suggest intercessory prayer, a pick-me-up, penance, therapy, evening classes in theology or a milky drink at night. All these she waves aside, and asks, surprised, if you are not losing sleep too?

You try to point out, as tactfully as you can, that after a day of hospital visiting, and hospices, and people with problems of rehousing, and marriage breakdowns, your sleep is not going to be disturbed by biblical criticism, higher or lower.

But you can learn a lot at parties – all the subtle things that no text-book can ever teach you. At Oxford I didn't get much out of the lectures. They were very clever, but cleverness was nothing new. There had been lots of it in the poverty of Stepney. As a child I knew geniuses, poets who slept on park benches, and rabbis who could work miracles (could you get cleverer than that?)

But it was at an Oxford party I learned something new. It was a very posh party and how I came to be invited to it I do not know. At that time, after the war, strapless dresses were in and the girls looked very delectable as they were twirled round and round in a fast waltz. But then disaster struck. A girl twirled, but her dress didn't. Quickly she left the floor.

'Poor girl,' I said to my partner, 'I'm sorry for her.'

'I don't know what you mean?' she answered.

'But you must have seen what happened,' I said, amazed.

'I saw nothing,' she repeated. 'I do not know what you are talking about.'

'But you must have seen her.' I was quite annoyed.

'A lady only sees what she is supposed to see,' she answered in a clipped voice, 'and only knows what she is supposed to know and I suggest you do the same.'

Well, I got Honours in history, but barely a pass as an English Gentleman. There was obviously a lot more study ahead and I would have to go to more parties.

Your Last Judgement

Like a lot of Jewish people I wear my shroud on the Day of Atonement because it is a sort of rehearsal for my own demise, followed by my Last Judgement, and my entry into kingdom come. On that day 'everything is off, dear' as the waitresses used to say in austerity years, stocks and shares, sex, sin and sausages, all food, all drink, all business, all entertainment. You mustn't even cheat and swallow your tooth water, though I think the Talmud says if you are mad enough to swallow a mouthful of pepper God may not hold it against you.

Well, if everything else is off, what's on? Non-stop liturgy with prayers, psalms and sermons, leading into even more sermons, psalms and prayers. If you think you've prayed before, you've got another thought coming. You pray for sins you've committed, for sins you haven't, for sins you've never thought of, and for some so bizarre I still don't know what they mean. I remember as a child that the liturgy provided a liberal education, getting to places ordinary school teachers could never reach, and informing you of things your best friends didn't dare tell you (probably because they didn't know them either).

As for me, my voice goes after the first two hours of the liturgy. It is then replaced by a squeak which though nasty is quite serviceable, and audible to the back row. I don't give a thought to food during the day but sometimes I have to push a cup of tea out of my mind.

I like the Day of Atonement; I even enjoy it. Death is a fact of life. It seems you don't have one without the other, so it's good to get in a bit of practice and prepare yourself in time – rehearse for the forthcoming and inevitable scenario.

A Christian friend told me of this incident at his church, and I've always kept it in mind. Hardly anybody turned up for a service there one cold winter evening. My friend apologised to the priest, pointing out that the weather that day was dreadful etc., etc. The priest listened impassively and then said in a dry, courteous voice, 'There is no guarantee, Mr So-and-so, that the Day of Judgement will be fine either.'

Since nothing is exempt from Jewish humour, not even the Fast itself, here is one of those stories of Judgement that go the rounds of Jewish communities.

A Jewish worthy of impeccable piety was tempted to

play golf on the morning of the Day of Atonement. Unable to resist temptation, he stole away to the golf course at dawn when no one was about and tried the first hole. He was astonished to get it in two. The second he holed in one. His astonishment and elation grew as he went round the course needing only one or two shots per hole.

The angels in heaven looked down, saw what was going on, and were thoroughly indignant about it. They trooped to the Holy One Blessed be He, and lodged a complaint. How could such a sinner be allowed to triumph in this way? It was a cosmic scandal.

God, however, appeared quite relaxed about it, so they complained again, crosser than ever, demanding divine punishment on the reprobate.

'Of course,' said God, 'of course, but don't you see? Who can he tell it to?'

In case the Last Judgement terrifies you, I give you this forecast of it, given to me by my teacher. 'All that will happen,' he said, 'is that God will put you on his knee (so to speak) and tell you what your life was about. You will see it then without illusion, and that will be your heaven and your hell.'

Self Honesty

When I first came to religion I wanted to know more about God because I was frightened of knowing too much about myself. Lots of people use piety to evade or avoid. But as the kingdom of heaven is within you, you can't know one without knowing the other, and if you try it produces some strange and nasty results such as fanaticism, holy wars, and persecution. The doubts we suppress inside ourselves become the 'heretics' we suppress in the world outside.

I've ruminated a lot about my own life, partly because I am self-absorbed like most pious people and partly because I want to locate the divinity within me and not just another hang up.

It is tempting to leave out the sex bit, and the silly bit, but the result would be too sanitary and false. I rely on religion to help me not to be sensitively selective. I may pretend I am only trying to protect religion, the truth is I am only protecting me.

God of the clumsy and the incompetent

I have always been a clumsy person, and to this day (I say it to my shame) I look helplessly at plugs and cannot change a fuse. Perhaps that was why I went into religion – not being very competent with the things of this world it seemed prudent to specialise in the affairs of the next.

I remember the horror of swimming lessons at school.

Swimming was fine, and undressing I could manage, but dressing was a different matter. I gazed helplessly at all the openings and holes in my underwear and wondered where did I put what? This incompetence caused even more confusion at puberty.

At school at the end of the war all the boys were instructed in darning. The cat's-cradle of threads was quite beyond me, and I just sewed up the holes. The result was painful and I had to walk around on points. 'Does he take dancing lessons?' said one aunt incredulously.

When I decided to take up sailing my nearest and dearest nearly ended up in hospital, or worse. I had by now matured and could distinguish left and right because you write with your write hand (or is it the left?) and also appeared to have mastered port and starboard. But windward and leeward was the straw that broke me and I proudly steered towards Norway, though we were making for Ostend.

In Malta I felt much at home because I met lots of people there who couldn't tell their right from their left and had to turn this way and that to give directions, as if they were doing a tango without the music.

The result of these limitations is that I am attracted not to perfect people or snob saints, but to those who trip up and wobble, who open their mouths and put their foot in it.

There was the nice refugee rabbi of my childhood who assured the congregation that he would look after their children from their infancy to their adultery. Knowing what I know now, perhaps he did!

I sympathise with the curate whose church was visited by Dean Inge when he was Dean of St Paul's. After listening to the sermon, the Dean called the curate to him. 'Mr So-and-so,' he said, 'how do you prepare your sermons?' The curate answered proudly, 'The first part,

140

Dean, I carefully work out myself, but the second part I leave to the inspiration of the Holy Ghost.'

'H'm,' said Dean Inge, 'I hope you won't think me blasphemous, Mr So-and-so, but I prefer your part.'

I always think of the Dean as I pass St Paul's on my way to Aldgate. My parents wanted me to speak posh, so I chose my words carefully – too carefully. It was the Dean who cured me. He came out with the following line.

'Whom are you?' he said, for he had been to evening classes.

After that I preferred to remain clumsy and never tried to talk posh again.

Blue unmasked

One of the most difficult things to believe is that God loves us as we are – not because of what we might become, or what we might achieve. It's difficult to get used to the idea because His love is so different from human love, where even the nicest people manipulate us or shove us around a bit. Even if it's for our own good, they still want something from us, or want us to perform for them. This means that their love is never really freely given. The strings may be difficult to spot but they are there.

As a result life forces us to wear lots of masks just to keep the peace. There is the mask we wear for our employers and the mask we wear for our employees. There is the mask we wear for those we love and the mask we wear for those we hate. And there is the mask we put on for prayer. Of course, there shouldn't be a mask for prayer, because God loves us as we are. But wearing a mask has become a habit – and it's terrifying to break.

People say it's difficult to know God. I've never found it so. God has remained pretty steady since we first got acquainted. It's the 'me' I find difficult to understand – the real me – because my masks have confused me so much.

In old Hebrew prayer books the word 'me' was printed in big letters at the beginning of the service because unless you got that sorted out, the following prayers remained unreal. I've been trying to sort out the real me from all the false 'mes' so that the real me can say a real prayer.

Take writing, for example. My teachers told me that to write or study I must go to a library and, amid all that high-class hush, I'd lay a cultured egg. Well, the silence just drove me round the bed. You know what it's like – somebody coughs and the cough goes round the world. I've never known such a place for creative constipation.

The real me, I've found, actually likes writing in buffet bars at railway stations, in hospital waiting rooms, and above all going round and round on the Circle line. As, physically, I am not travelling anywhere, I don't get rattled when the train is stuck in a tunnel. In fact, watching other people watching their watches gives me a lot of spiritual thoughts for the day – gratis. And I like the regular, soothing noise of the automatic doors.

Because I write on cookery, people tell me I must dote on *Cuisine Minceur*, soufflés and other high-rise creations. Well, I like them well enough but when I am out of England the real me craves for bangers, with brown sauce, in yeast extract gravy.

At the college where I teach, people point to learned articles and say, 'You've read this of course. What do you think about it?' Well, I try not to think about it because I don't like unhappy endings and an awful lot of Christian theology and Jewish history is about misery.

As for humour, being a Balliol man I ought to sniff and savour the sayings of La Rochefoucauld and other up-market bitchery. And I do, I do. It is, I agree, quite *quelque chose* – which means, as your French may not be up to much, quite something. But I also like *autre chose* too, which means something quite off. And what follows is a good example of what the real me really enjoys.

In Africa, some anthropologists heard of a tribe which every few years performed the mysterious butcher dance. Hacking their way through the jungle they located the tribe and asked the Chief if they could record it. 'Sure,' he said, 'but we do it every other year and last night was the night.'

They stayed for two years, waiting to witness the butcher dance, and when the time came, as dusk approached, they set up their cameras and tape recorders. Gravely, in the twilight, the tribe joined hands in a great circle. Then the Chief shouted, 'The butcher dance'. Everyone extended first a foot and then a hand into the magic circle and as the cameras whirred they began to chant, 'You putcha right foot in, you putcha right foot out!'

Well, that's the real me, and you may well prefer a refined mask. But this is the one that God created and He loves me as I am.

Stepmother nature

I never thought I would like growing old. But to my surprise my fifties are nicer than my forties and my forties nicer than my thirties and as for the twenties and the teens they were hell, and I certainly wouldn't wish them on a dog and probably not on my enemies either.

I suppose the real pleasure of age is that you are relieved from expectation. You don't have to prove yourself to anybody, or achieve anything.

As a result you can be honest with yourself, and admit to the things you really enjoy and not to the things you ought to enjoy. This makes life a lot smoother.

I can now admit my lapses of taste. I used to pretend to like nature, and I suppose I do – in parks and such, but being a Londoner I am quite satisfied with substitutes and for me Hampstead Heath is a good stand-in for the wide open spaces.

The only garden I ever really worked at was on the Med and I became very fond of it. I got the idea during a long, hot summer when nothing grew in the parched heat. In the morning from my balcony I used to hear a whirring sound which I took to be crickets but was actually vacuum cleaners. To make up for the deficiencies of nature, my fellow villagers had planted plastic flowers in pots and sprayed them with after-shave, which accounted for the confusing but romantic atmosphere at sunset time.

Olde-worlde ivy (in one-metre lengths) festooned the rustic bar and barbecue and English spring flowers were clipped on to the plastic grass with clothes pegs. Visitors did not water my garden but sprayed it with bottle ends of perfume.

It was, I admit, confusing to sniff lily of the valley that smelled of roses, and roses saturated with Blue Grass, but as booze was cheap and we spent our time tottering from one party to another, nobody got it straight. The only thing to remember was not to forget yourself and greet the dawn by dancing joyously in bare feet on the lawn. If you did, you had to take sticking plaster to bind your lacerations together and keep your gore from dripping on the aforesaid lily of the valley and direct it over red flowers like 'geraniums' or 'roses' instead.

I sometimes think of my little garden as I travel through the Midlands on an InterCity. Sometimes the train comes to a halt by a garden which gives me such pleasure it makes me exclaim 'Oh my!' in delight.

It is filled with concrete and polystyrene artefacts. Breeze block bunnies nibble composition pixies on stone mushrooms, and glass fibre fairies dance at the bottom of the garden.

My fellow travellers may sniff but I would like to get off and give the gardener a helping hand and spray Brut over his 'begonias'.

DUN WEEDIN'

And it's the same with many other enjoyments besides gardens. I used to force myself to sit through sombre films in which everyone was going to the dogs. Now I trot off to films about dogs instead, provided they have happy endings. I also used to wear myself out giving elaborate dinner parties to people I hardly knew (what on earth was I trying to prove?) Now one or two friends drop in for supper. We eat it in the kitchen and sometimes we put on the style, but quite often we satisfy a childhood craving for tinned pilchards and cocoa.

Though I work on liturgy for my community, my own prayers get shorter and shorter. I don't go in any more for '–ests' and '–eths', I just say, 'Lord, over to You' or 'Sorry'.

New fits and starts

The Jewish New Year has gone and I am thinking of all the fresh starts I'd like to make in life if I had the courage.

I am writing this in a train and I would like to get off at any station which attracts me or makes me curious and 'waste' a day taking unknown buses to unknown hamlets. Perhaps I'll meet someone. Who knows? I might even meet myself.

I'd like to make a party and invite all the friends I haven't heard of for the last twenty or thirty years. We might not have parted on very good terms but I have long ago forgotten what the quarrels were all about and I am curious to see what happened to them. Also, from the look in their eyes, I might find out what's happened to me in those years.

I'd like to take advantage of one of those long package deals you read about in the travel brochures. Now I'm over fifty-five, I feel important as I am entitled to an introductory dance, a free glass of Spanish champagne, a cookery demonstration and bingo. In my declining years I shall also qualify for tea and biscuits on the house, which will nourish me against the ravages of old age.

I'm not being snooty, I would really enjoy it, and though you need more than an old age pension to enjoy such treats, you don't need that much. In any case, excited by bingo and with stars in my eyes from the introductory dance, I should try my hand at a romantic novel. I have always been partial to happy endings and can never get enough of them. I don't mean refined happy endings, when the heroine is fulfilled as she faints away from famine or the hero chortles manfully as he is redeemed by renunciation, but real happy endings when they all merrily marry each other and receive lovely presents and get spirituality, sex and financial security (bingo!) for ever and ever. Amen.

There never seem to be enough of such endings in life or on bookshelves so I shall write my own with a pencil in an exercise book. My imagination will bubble from my free glass of Spanish champagne and now that I am well past pimples and puberty the love interest will be absorbing without driving me crazy.

I also want to try out a new type of spirituality. I've got a book on retreat centres and it affects me like a box of Black Magic chocolates. I should like to taste the spiritual treats provided there and have a bite at divine delights I've never yet got my teeth into. What is a preached retreat? Do we all give sermons to each other? Not at breakfast, surely! Now, how about a week of total silence? Well, why not? But is there central heating? Ah, pity, we'll have to stay in the world instead.

But I really would like a good pray-out. You never get the chance if you're a minister. It's always 'five minutes and you're on' or the clerical version thereof, and you have to organise your thoughts in sermons and not let them dribble around your mind.

I'd also like to give up cooking for a month. I've been so busy trying out recipes, tasting them and testing them that I just want to live on convenience foods for a while (nut milk chocolate and smoked salmon) and throw my casserole with my right hand over my left shoulder. I should love to say I cannot be parted from my rolling pin but I can and you can have it (on loan for a month).

I'd like to pick up a paper and be merry as I read the front page. Couldn't they put cookery and bridge and Princess Michael and such on the front page and relegate the political dinosaurs to the spaces in between your stars and the unit trusts?

I'd better stop as I'm getting frivolous and people do like their ministers weighty, woolly perhaps, but wise and weighty. Can I have my glass of Spanish champagne, please?

A confusion

The liturgy warned us that before we went to bed at night the devil, like a roaring lion, was prowling around the priory and was out to get us. Give him an inch and we'd had it.

By the devil I suppose they meant sex, because when nocturnal sins are not specified by saintly people it's even stevens they mean fornication.

I felt aggrieved because speaking personally I've never found such pleasures as easy as the liturgy suggests. I get too nervous. As my piano teacher said when we parted, at his request, for ever, 'Lionel, my boy, you just haven't got the touch.'

This judgement was confirmed in puberty when I tried to find out about 'Life' in the back rows of cinemas. I've never been very good at tying knots at sea or untying them on land and a cat's-cradle of tapes, buttons, and sneaky bits of elastic separated me from that lion of lust.

It was such tough going I thought I'd get more pleasure from popcorn. So did my girlfriend, who said if this was love it was more like a red cross lesson with tourniquets. We munched our way thoughtfully through a Tarzan film, rather worried because we felt we had failed our eleven plus in life studies.

Sin wasn't nearly as easy as religious people think. Even when I thought I'd made it in a maize field on a work camp I got interrupted by a goat, who chased me through the stalks.

It was this early frustration which made me so sympathetic to an elderly man who told me he wanted to propose to a lady much younger. Yes, he loved her. No, he didn't want one of those companionate marriages which are regarded as sensible for the old. He wanted all the pleasures I had longed for in the back row.

Did the lady want him? I asked. Yes, of course, he said, otherwise he wouldn't be wasting my time. Then what was the problem?

Courage, he said. He had had little experience, and you need a lot of courage to strip physically and emotionally in front of another person. It needs a lot of trust to expose your superfluous hair to someone else. You need so much listening and understanding to lead someone else into happiness. He had thought of the ministry once, but contemplation and prayer were never as tough as this.

Yes, he would need a lot of courage, I thought, because the world is not kind to older people in love. They are called 'cradle snatchers' if they are women, and the men 'old goats'. But I blessed him and wished him good luck and told him to pop the question. Yes, there would be problems. But all the experience of plain speaking in prayer would come to his aid in bed too. The same courage is required to expose one's nakedness and one's needs in both places.

There's an awful misunderstanding going on. A lot of people come to religion asking one sort of question but we answer instead another question which is easier for us. They ask, 'How can I be happy?', and we tell them how they can be good. But I think both questions are fair. If faced honestly both lead to the same reality and integrity. I understood why he felt shy about speaking to his own minister.

The confusion is rather like that in the Jewish story of the man who dropped down, seemingly dead, in the street.

'A doctor, a doctor,' his wife called.

A doctor bent over him and said gravely, 'I'm afraid your husband is dead, Mrs Cohen.'

At this point the husband's body started to twitch and the husband whispered, 'No, no, I'm alive, I'm alive.'

'Be quiet,' said his wife, 'and listen to the doctor.'

Heppiness

Next Monday, I'll be in Spain on a package holiday. I've been looking forward to it for weeks and reading through the travel brochure over and over again. I've bought a pair of trendy white pants in a sale, which are daring and a little bit see-through, and a trendy vest with more holes than fabric.

All I need is a rest, not a vest, but I also want a change of character too. For two weeks I don't want to be a middle-aged rabbi. I'd like to be one of the beautiful people who live in my dreams and fantasies.

But my holidays don't work out – they can't because I've never been honest about my own happiness. My white pants are thirty-one-inch leg and thirty-six-inch waist; the leg is honest, the waist is not. I breathed in while I was being measured and on full board I won't be able to suck in my breath any more, without risking cardiac arrest. The vest is also very fetching – but on someone else, the fantasy me. Who on earth would want to peer through the holes to the grey and grisly mattress beneath?

At a certain point in life we all have to become friends

with ourselves as we are. It isn't easy and I had to comfort a fellow clergyman whose dream was also broken rather brutally.

He had plucked up courage and against his wife's advice slipped into a trendy outfitters in the West End. He coveted a pair of pale blue stretch pants in the window. Just as he was easing himself into them he heard two assistants talking. One said to the other, 'That's a brave bit of mutton.' In a frenzy of embarrassment he peeled off the pants and rushed to the door. But that provided no escape, for his wife sharply turned him round and sent him racing back to the changing room – for the combination of dog collar and underbriefs is not acceptable even in Oxford Street.

Why do we kid ourselves with such fibs, for they are too pathetic to be called lies? Why do grown-up adults like us play such childish games?

I think it is because at first the real rules of happiness seem very hard – so frightening that we shelter in fantasy.

Firstly, the best way to happiness is to forget it. When you run after it, it runs after you and you end up chasing after your own tail. But if you can forget it, one grey Monday morning when you don't expect it you'll wake up and say, 'Good Lord, I'm happy!' You don't need a holiday to step into heaven. It opens up more easily to you when you give up your seat in a crowded bus or sit quietly on a park bench after a day at work.

Second lesson. Happiness is a by-product of giving and giving up. Only when you can freely give what you have, and freely give up what you are, can you cut down the sadness in your life. Sooner or later everything we receive has to be given back to our Creator. It is better to get in some practice now and learn to do it with good grace, not with groans.

A third lesson. Be careful where you put your heart,

for everything and everybody changes, and if they break, your heart will be broken too. It is only safe to invest your heart in that which never changes: God or God in them.

But though such lessons seem very hard, you can learn them without feeling too heavy, dear. Old Jewish stories help them down, because our fathers never took happiness too seriously – it wasn't the purpose of our life on earth.

Two holidaymakers in a crowded plane were disturbed to hear an old man crying in the seat behind them. 'Oy, oy, I'm so unheppy,' he wailed, 'oy, oy, I'm so unheppy!' They couldn't stand it. They turned round and did all they could for the old man. They gave him a cushion and a cup of tea and a newspaper and were settling back to enjoy their drink when the crying started all over again.

'Oy, oy I'm so heppy,' he wailed 'oy, oy I'm so heppy, oy, oy I'm so heppy!'

Common-sense cordon Blue

I cannot be an agony aunt because I am the person who has the problems, not the one who solves them. Yes, I do know quite a lot about counselling and therapy and all that but I have not learned it looking superior and sitting in a chair with a notepad but by lying on a couch, feeling flat in every sense.

But if you want to share problems and solutions, here goes. Here is a worm's eye view of wisdom, common-sense cordon Blue.

If you wake up at an impossible time in the night don't start counting sheep or jumping over stiles. They will only make you think of farmers' subsidies and the Common Market, and this will make you morose and you will want to jump off a butter mountain into a wine lake – if you know how to get to them, that is. (Isn't it odd how everybody says they exist, but nobody seems to know where? Can you buy a day return to look at them?)

Instead, don't feel guilty about not sleeping. After all, though there's lots of things in your life you should feel guilty about, now is not the time or place, and why add to the real crosses you have to bear some fiendish plastic ones of your own devising?

A nice thing to do at night is to tidy up a drawer, reading all the old papers in it and tearing them up. Sometimes among the debris you will find a bit of chocolate. It looks a bit beige around the edges but it tastes nice if you suck it.

As you suck it you can ponder old letters. 'How could you have done this to me?' starts one of them. Well, this is too strong stuff for night time and in any case you can't remember who 'me' is. As time has presumably healed all, tear up the letter and have a gulp of cocoa or cooking sherry to steady yourself.

Occasionally you find a peseta or a drachma among the debris and this makes you feel good, as if Providence has smiled on you. (It hasn't.)

Quite often, though, your worries will cancel each other out. Say you think you are going to expire tomorrow and you are also worried because you've got marge not butter for your dinner party and will people notice. Well, if you're only going to be present at the dinner party in spirit, does marge matter?

In the middle of the night I enjoy telling myself very old and very corny jokes, which I like but never dare tell in public. You know the sort. A guy from Manchester (not London, of course) comes back from a holiday in

Italy, rushes home, and as he opens the door shouts, 'Mam, I'm 'ere.' Get it?

Perhaps I'd better stop now. You've had enough wisdom at one go and you might start throwing things.

'Innocent' exercise

Being a rather ungainly child I never took to the gymnasium at school. If I could, I squeezed between the wall bars and the wall to keep out of sight and this did nicely, until I grew fatter and couldn't get out. While my contemporaries leapt over the 'horse' like gazelles, I could only butt it like a goat and I was the one concussed, not the 'horse'.

I also dreaded the changing room, because not having brothers or sisters I was very shy at my nakedness, and I was also very clumsy. It took me a long time to tie shoelaces, and I still sometimes have to knot them as my recognition of right and left is dodgy.

But the school doctor was adamant: some exercise I must have, though he kindly said I could choose my own.

I first decided on tap dancing and joined an academy where I brought up the end of a long line of 'hoofers'. It was 1940 so we waved our arms in the air to 'Hang out the washing on the Siegfried Line', and I tried to look saucy as I sang tremulously 'You can't black out the moon'. There was a war on and entertainment was scarce, so I had a modest success in the remoter reaches of Dartmoor. I was very chubby and sang 'The nightingale sang in Berkeley Square' with a Yiddish Cockney accent, and this wowed them in the depths of Devon.

When it became clear that they were laughing at me

not with me, I switched from art to ideology and told the doctor I was taking up marching to avoid infantile obesity.

I had always been unprincipled as far as marching was concerned. Give me a good beat and a banner, with a bun to eat at the end, and I was anybody's. In the Popular Front days before the war in the East End of London I had marched for Stalin, for Trotsky, and Edward the Eighth. Why the last? you might ask. Why any of them? I answer.

When I was evacuated the banner had different words but the beat was still 'om pom pom' and you still got a bit of bun even though there was a war on. I marched now for our Empire on which the sun never set (you could see it in pictures on rare tins of pineapple). I also marched for decency and against drink.

Occasionally, of course, we met rival marchers who

were against the revolution, the Empire, and decency, and there was a confrontation.

A lot of politics is ritual these days, exercise in role playing. Your opponents, with whom you have a lot in common, must be villains (otherwise you would not allow yourself a satisfying release of aggression). Also the villainy on your own side must be glossed over (otherwise you would be deprived of the glow which comes from solidarity). Recently a very worthy cause I know wanted to mobilise children's power and organise a march. I am not easily shocked but I am when children are lured with lollipops into ideology or politics. The best that can result is pop; the worst is teaching tots to become cannon fodder.

I once took part in a demonstration to focus attention on the plight of homeless pussies. Because I couldn't find anybody to look after her my dog Re'ach came too. Like me she loved the beat, and the banner and the bun, and bowwowed in support.

Like lots of demonstrators she never (thank God) understood the purpose only the pleasure of the march. She would have marched just as happily for Stalin, Trotsky, the Empire, decency, drink – and, of course, the Nazis.

Last thoughts

Had a cold and on the doctor's orders go for an X-ray. Stand stripped to the waist in a weedy line with others at the hospital. Bad for morale. We look like pigeons who have traded in their breast feathers for inadequate lumps of fur.

Remembered that when I was ill as a child Granny

gave me instant rum and an amulet, packed with psalms like batteries in a transistor – much more comforting.

We are X-rayed and told to go home, but I am also told to come back after lunch, and not to worry. I gobble two portions of curry and rice to show I am not worrying.

After lunch I return and my chest is X-rayed again from many angles. Staff and students purse their lips and leave me filed away on a padded shelf. I artfully trap a ward orderly who is trying to take a short cut on tiptoe without being noticed.

I turn on the pressure and he tells all. There is a big black mark on the plate. Is it a growth or a hole? He doesn't know but thinks it's a hole and tells me not to worry.

Now is the time for the consolation of religion! I take a Bible from my briefcase and self-consciously open it at random. All I get is the end of the story of Jezebel, where the dogs will soon lick her blood. It is not appropriate in my situation so I read some copies of women's magazines instead, and am much cheered.

But I feel alone and panicky. Suddenly tearful, realise that I've been offered everything I ever wanted in life, including companionship, but threw it away. Wasn't cheated, just silly. God not responsible.

What about the afterlife then? Do I believe in my own religion? The crunch comes. I decide I do in the main and am relieved. Now see the point of all those duty prayers and services I've recited. They trained me to see the unseen at work inside myself and others. Glad that a bit of me is familiar with eternity – makes it easier for the rest of me to catch up.

But what will it be like? Remember Abelard who said 'heaven is where you get everything you want and it will be as lovely as when you still wanted it.'

If that's what it's going to be like I can't wait to get there – though on reflection, I can.

158

But what about the other place – if it exists? I remember that Mother Julian, who was a mystic, was given a tour of hell in the Middle Ages. 'It was empty,' she reported 'there wasn't even a Jew there.'

Now what a nice lady. I wonder if Grandma would have approved of her. Suddenly realise I may find out sooner than I expect.

The door opens and my ward orderly comes back and tells me I can dress. 'You can go now,' he says kindly, 'and you don't have to come back.' No prescription necessary. No explanation given. He tells me not to worry.

In case it worries you, all this happened many years ago and I am still alive and well and worrying now about other things.